I AM MARKED

I AM MARKED

E.J. EDEN

pink elephant
PRESS

DEDICATION

To all the girls who believe they can't;
Actually, you can.

The only thing necessary for the triumph of evil
is for good men to do nothing.

EDMUND BURK

CHAPTER

ONE

I hadn't planned on dying today.

But as I turn to see the Mute that's behind me, I know it's inevitable. This enemy is huge. Dangerous. Ruthless. Usually I can take that kind of thing down easily.

If I had more than one knife.

And if it didn't have two heads.

In less than a second it's a few feet in front of me. It's faster than me — much faster. Running isn't an option.

I dive out of the way just before its yellowing teeth snap into my torso. Its reptilian eyes sear into mine. My speed is close to its own — I guess I'm not the easy meal it's used to. We begin slowly circling each other, both assessing the same thing: who will strike next.

The small girl I saw just moments ago appears in my mind. I wonder if she managed to elude this monster or if it already devoured her before I arrived. My stomach turns at the thought.

It lunges for me but I evade the blow just in time. I aim for its heart, throwing my knife with every ounce of strength I have left. The knife bounces off the scales onto the ground a few metres away.

Shit.

Well I guess its scales are pretty hard then.

The Mute bristles in anger at the attempt on its life. I jump high into the air, channelling all of my energy into a strike at its head. My own mutations kick in and the sharp pain at the end of my toes tells me I might have just grown some claws of my own. The Mute howls in pain as my claws hit home in one of its eyes. It stumbles back on its hind legs in agony.

The Mute rallies and attacks in a fury. I attempt to roll out of its way and land on my feet in anticipation of the next attack, but my footing is all wrong. I am unfamiliar with my newfound claws and I stumble ever so slightly in an attempt to regain my balance. The Mute now has that millisecond while I'm distracted and uses it well.

I see claws. I hear something tear.

Unimaginable pain bursts through my body. My vision is blurry. The world is just lumps of colour and nothing else. I scream in agony.

I stagger and fall to the ground. My fingers grab at the overgrown grass, the cold mud forcing my palms to slip, sending me flailing. I attempt to crawl away from its jaws, from the final blow that it will send to kill me.

Through the blur of pain, I see blonde hair emerge from the clearing. It sounds like Skyler, screaming my name.

"Run—" It's all I manage to get out as I taste the salty blood in my mouth beginning to choke me. Skyler's screams have drawn the attention of the Mute and it rounds on her, furious to be distracted at the opportune moment.

My ears sting at a new noise, unfamiliar and terrifying and wonderful all at the same time.

I think it must be the loudest thing I've ever heard. Is it coming from behind Skyler? Other humans emerge from the tree line holding black objects. They blur in and out of my vision.

And then the lumps of colour form into a boy – no – a man. He's walking towards me.

I haven't seen a man other than Dad for years. But it can't possibly be a man because I'm dying. It must be an angel. He leans over me.

Strangely, I'm not scared of the angel. He's come to take me home. To Mum. The colours around me fade again. I'm so tired. The angel's eyes sear into mine, round pools of amber and molten honey.

He shakes me hard.

"Hang on," he says.

Hang on to what? I want to reply, but all that comes out is air. Or does he say that? Or am I dreaming?

I am shaking and I don't know why. Did something just happen?

I trust the amber eyes.

I will be safe now.

The world descends into darkness.

TWO

Strange sounds. White sheets. Red bandages. Gasping breaths. Pain. A dark man. White light. Attempts to breathe. Gasping. Reaching. Beeping sounds. Plastic tubes. Choking. More blood. Black and red. Amber. A dark man watching me. Amber eyes gone again. Darkness.

1641

I vomit as I wake because there's something stuck, something down my throat. I retch. A man in a white suit is at the edge of my bed. He shouts at a lady in a pale dress who pulls the strange tube from my throat. I can breathe now. *But where am I?* I scream for Skyler. Someone tries to hold me down but I buck and break from them. Behind me, I feel a sting as the lady pushes a thin silver spear into my arm. It stings. The man in the suit looks bored.

4

1641

The next time I open my eyes, it's lighter than it was before. There is something attached to the roof above me and it blinds me as I stare at it. It hurts as much as when I look directly into the sun. I feel a slight pain in my wrist. I look to the problem and see there is a metal binding there, tying my arm to the bed.

"A precaution, of course."

A voice descends from a corner in the room. The sun in the ceiling is so bright, it's blinding me. I blink again, disorientated, but I can only make out a figure of a man, nothing more. "Even in your weakened state, your outburst managed to knock my Guardian out and give him a decent black eye in the process."

Guardian?

"I don't remember th—"

He chuckles and steps into the light. It's White Suit Man. Probably double my age. Stocky. Handsome maybe, if it weren't for the scar that pulls one side of his face into a permanent grimace.

"I see you're feeling better, Ava."

"How the hell do you know my—"

"Skyler, of course."

He senses my panic and holds out his palms to me slightly, shaking his head and smiling. I wonder if this is his attempt at being friendly. It looks odd.

"Don't worry, she's safe. She took quite a fright when that organism almost killed you."

Organism? Does he mean that Mute?

"Where's Skyler?" I look around the room but can't see any trace of her. I can't even smell her scent.

"You're lucky to be alive. Thank goodness we had our specialized team of nurses to take good care of you."

What the hell is a nurse?

"Who are you?" The longer I can stall him, the longer I have to figure out an escape route.

The room is grey. All grey. I feel cold.

I am attached to a machine that beeps a lot.

I glance around and notice there are no windows. How high are we from the ground? I figure jumping isn't an option. The only way out is through this man, and he is blocking the exit. My fist tenses in anticipation of the fight.

"Why, you're a feisty young thing, aren't you? Intelligent too. I can see you've clocked your only exit." He grins at me. That looks odd too. "Listen, Ava, focus here just for a moment, will you? I have a proposition for you."

He sits on the bed, a few centimetres away from me, seemingly pleased by my own displeasure.

He smells artificial. It's a strong musk, I haven't smelt anything like that before. His impenetrable gaze makes nerves fizz through every corner of my body. I am on fire under those eyes. He is burning me alive.

"You have a family, yes?"

My eyes widen in disbelief. "How do you know th—"

"Like I said, Skyler has been a great ally to me already. She is not part of your family though?"

"N—No." I stutter. "I ... I saved her. A few years back."

"I see. But you have a younger brother, yes? Xander."

I tense as my little brother's name rolls off this strange man's tongue with such familiarity.

"Just eight years old. How sweet. And a father?"

I don't move or say a word.

"And your mother is...?"

"Dead." I say unflinchingly, without missing a beat.

"I see." He clasps his hands in front of him and takes a few steps toward me. I try to shuffle away from him but my bindings won't let me.

"Ava, I am the elected leader of a new community. A place that began to form before the Cull, twenty years ago. We call it Haven."

"That's impossible. No one knew the Cull was coming."

"Is it, Ava?" he asks.

"You're saying someone ... some people ... knew that it was going to happen?"

"They didn't just know. They planned it. A select percentage was to be infected. It was either that or certain death for all. The strain that humans had put on the planet's resources was ... just tremendous. What they didn't account for, though, was the strength of the virus they released. It infected us all."

He grins again. I don't know why he keeps doing that. The scar running down his face looks slightly wet, like it's oozing blood.

"When the disease had mutated beyond their control, they decided to bring the best minds together in a corner far away from the rest of the world: New Zealand. One of those minds happened to be mine."

His eyes glow with pride and ... something else. Something I can't quite place.

"They hid us. We were to be the saviours of the human race. We were to deliver Earth to a new age. The new Moses, Noah, or even Jesus, if you will."

I frown at these foreign names.

I struggle with my bonds on the bed. My adapts should have kicked in by now, and I'd be strong enough to break them and run. Or my body would do something else, something to make me a predator again, not the prey. But it hadn't. Why weren't my adapts kicking in?

He continues, either ignoring my quiet struggle or too wrapped up in his own story to pay attention: "But the disease had a life of its own. It's all we could do to protect ourselves from it. We *all* were lucky enough to mutate."

"How do I know you're telling the truth?" I ask.

He chuckles and tucks a strand of hair behind my ear. I go to bite him. He can get the *hell* off.

"I won't hurt you." He croons, as if comforting a wounded animal, "That hair ... so strange. You remind me of..." He trails off and his eyes become haunted. As if he's seeing someone else before him, not me. He blinks and the vacant look in his eyes is gone.

He is back in the room.

"Forgive me, Ava."

"It's fine."

It's really not fine.

Why do I feel so cold?

"You just ... look so much like ... no matter. From our research, we discerned that most humans have mutated with sensory improvement, physical improvement and less need for sustenance and rest. But you, Ava ... you're different. You're special. In the twenty years since the Cull, I've never seen anything like you. But I think you already know that, don't you?"

He leans toward me again. I avert his eyes at all costs.

How does he know about me? Did Skyler tell him?

This is bad. This is very, very bad.

"Ava, listen to me. I don't want to use you, as I suspect others might have in the past. I want to help you."

"I don't need your help." I say, a little more confidently than I feel.

I shiver at the thought of that reptile Mute. If those humans with the black objects hadn't interceded, I would probably be dead by now.

"The Chosen will help you make your family safe again."

He seems to enjoy his explanation. He seems to like the sound of his voice.

"We saved you from that organism, with something called a gun. Guns are a rarity these days, but a rarity we possess nevertheless. Mutes cannot enter Haven. We have the resources to keep them out. Haven could be your home too, if you wanted."

My breath catches. I remember Dad telling me about those things called guns. These people have the ability to kill Mutes easily. We haven't been able to find any guns since the Cull. Ever.

So, the Chosen had rounded up all of the guns, then. No more knives bouncing off scales. No more arrows. I smile as I imagine the burden being lifted off my shoulders. The burden of protecting my family at all costs has weighed heavily on me since Mum...

But *they* could protect us.

This could be our home.

Haven.

THREE

"Ava!" Skyler bursts into the room, all sunlight and smiles. She leaps onto the bed and hugs me fiercely. I grimace in pain but force a smile. White Suit Man left a few minutes ago. My head has been pounding ever since.

Her bright blue eyes are alight with excitement. I sigh in relief. I haven't been able to focus without her by my side. We haven't gone a day without seeing each other since I'd found her. That was about four years ago now, when she was just ten years old. Since her parents died at the claws of that Mute, she'd insisted I teach her everything I know about fighting, about hunting.

Just like Mum had taught me. Before ... well, before everything had changed.

The memory that invades my mind before I can shut it out: Mum, Dad, and eleven-year-old me, sparring and hunting together. It feels like a lifetime ago. So much has changed. Dad's leg is so ruined from that Mute attack, he can barely walk. And Mum ... I try to recall her face in my mind. The sharp jawline, the grey eyes, the long black hair. In my mind's eye, she's a bit blurry, as if I have forgotten some of her features. It gets harder to remember her face every day.

I shake the memories from my mind. She's gone. No use living in the past. It's done now.

Skyler holds me tightly as she erupts, "I can't believe you're here. You're alive! They said you were resting and I wasn't allowed to see you for two whole days and it's been driving me crazy! Did you hear about the Chosen? They are going to help us, we can stay here, in Haven! And I met Nancy and she's the nurse and she's really nice, and how's your back I heard it has a huge scar now and —"

"*What?*"

I stand up, flinching a little at the pain pulsing through my body. Across the room, I see my reflection on a wall, as if I were looking into the river on a sunny day. I am slimmer than I was the last time I saw myself. It had been a hard winter, and I'd always given my seconds to Xander, if we ever had any. My high cheekbones jut out prominently; my features were softer before, now they've become more angular and strained. My jet-black hair hangs to my shoulders and my grey eyes gaze back at me. My skin bears the memories of my fight, a few deep wounds carved over my body – there, on my arm, my collarbone. As I turn, I gasp in horror. Through the back of the thin robe I'm wearing I can see a three-claw mark stretching angrily from my shoulder blade all the way down, diagonally across my back.

Tears sting my eyes. I mean, it's stupid. It's selfish. I've had cuts before, but suddenly I feel marred. Broken.

"Nancy said you should be dead. That any other human, even after the Cull, should be dead." Her eyes roam over me in worry, and she squeezes my hand, as if to remind herself I'm still here.

"Skyler. What did you tell them about me?"

"Nothing. I mean, they kind of figured it out themselves. I think the people that saved you watched some of your fight with that Mute. And, I mean, look at you. It's not hard to figure out you're different from the rest of us."

I roll my eyes but even as I return to the mirror, I can see that she's right. Anyone else would have been killed by that blow. But the wound that must have been just two days old, looks as if it had been healing for a few weeks. Maybe even months.

I look at Skyler in the reflection, standing behind me. "You cut all your hair? Where's it gone, you're..."

"Bald. It's funny, right?" says Skyler rapidly. "If you're Marked, you have to shave your head. The Chosen – they're the ones in white. They tattoo us so they can keep track of how big the population is getting. And other things I'm pretty sure, but they haven't told me what yet. I've been in a holding room, too – they haven't let me see Haven just yet. But the nurse told me it's beautiful. And safe. No Mutes can get in here. And the Guardians are soldiers that protect us from any other threats."

She turns and sure enough, there on the nape of her neck is a black line of numbers: *1642*.

"Skyler, why did you let them do that to you?"

She shrugs nonchalantly. "I didn't have a choice really. They did it when I was unconscious. And to you, too."

I return to my reflection and pull my hair to the side. I have a matching tattoo on the nape of my neck. Just different numbers. *1641*. I seethe in silence looking at my Mark.

Skyler approaches me. "It's not too bad." She smiles and then her face crumples as I see the new thought in her eyes. She says quietly, "Why did you run, Ava? That day when we were on the hunt. I could have helped you with that Mute. We could have got it together. But you just ... took off. And I couldn't save you. You could have died."

Her eyes bear the guilt she no doubt felt and I hang my head in shame. She's right. It was stupid of me to run off like that.

An image of the girl swims into my mind. I close my eyes and return to that day. She needs to understand what happened. Why I ran.

"There was a girl."

1641

The hunt was going well. With a Mute similar to what they used to call a rabbit slung over each of our shoulders, we are in high spirits. We won't be going hungry tonight. We slip through the trees, disturbing nothing but the broken bark crunching quietly under the soles of our bare feet. Our feet are strong, our skin tough as leather. Most of the time we don't wear any coverings on our feet – shoes, as Dad calls them – unless we're hunting in Wellington, where the remnants of broken glass can cut us. We don't need that sort of thing out here.

The canopy of the trees above us throws shadows onto the fallen leaves below our feet. The wind picks up slightly and I can hear the rustle of smaller animals for miles around. As the breeze changes its direction, so do the sounds around us. I can now hear the rapid trickle of a stream; it sounds like a few kilometres away.

Skyler and I glance at each other, a slow grin spreading on both of our faces before we break into a run.

As we draw close to the happy chatter of the water, Skyler sprints harder, overtaking me, heading toward the river. She laughs as the freezing water hits her skin, and disappears under, looking for water Mutes. Fish, I remind myself. I need to start using the words Dad has been teaching me from the books before the Cull.

I kneel down on a rock, cupping my hands full of sweet the liquid and drink. The refreshing taste of nothingness soothes my swollen tongue. The ache of needing sustenance disappears.

I close my eyes as I dunk my sticky feet into the stream. The sun ventures down through the canopy of trees and hits the water with such magnificence, I almost gasp at the beauty of what is around me. A bird flits by, his third wing a colourful dorsal on his back. His head is bigger than the rest of his body, his eyes gigantic. He takes his own fill of the water before noticing me staring and disappears again.

I close my eyes. I breathe in the cool air. I feel alive.

Free.

And then, something breaks my reverie.

My head snaps up. My eyes scan the horizon deftly, my muscles leaping to attention. Adrenaline hits me, coursing through my veins with urgency. I'm ready to take down the threat.

I see what my senses have alerted me to. A few hundred metres away from me, hiding behind a tree, is a young girl. She stands quietly, watching me with a quizzical look on her face. Her hand is gently peeling off some bark from the tree. I can hear her nails scratch against it from here. Tiny and frail, she can't be more than seven.

I gasp but it's too late – she's seen me notice her. She turns on her heel and runs, disappearing out of sight. "NO!" I scream. I think it's the loudest noise I've ever made. "WAIT!"

Without a second thought, I begin to wade through the river, jumping up onto the bank to follow her. My body hums with electricity, at the thought of talking to her, asking her where her family lives, how they have survived this long.

Just an hour ago, I was arguing with Skyler about other humans. Just an hour ago, I had no need for them. It was better to keep our group small, I'd said to Skyler. Too many others and they'd put us all in danger. I'd made the decision we weren't going to go looking for others. We'd keep to our hunting ground, and not venture past it. That's the rule Mum had always given us. And I'd be damned if I didn't respect her wishes.

Now, here I am running after another human. Seeing this little girl has changed everything.

As I scramble through the stubborn bushes around me, I hear Skyler calling my name. I ignore her and continue my chase.

An absurd image of this small girl and Xander sword-fighting with small sticks appears in my mind. Xander with another child, eating together, being kids together...

I can give him a future. A friend, maybe. I can make him happy again.

I guess you don't realize how much you miss something until it's within your grasp. She is my chance. My chance at living. Finally living. Maybe they have a better way of protecting themselves against the Mutes. Maybe I won't have to live in fear every day for the rest of my life.

The trees begin to thin and I stop as I reach a clearing. Before me lies a small overgrown field, with trees around the entire perimeter. My ragged breathing breaks the deafening silence.

I can't hear Skyler's calls for me anymore. The sound of singing birds has gone. I can no longer hear the little girl's footsteps.

She's outrun me. I feel tears forming in my eyes, which is completely absurd. I didn't even know this girl; what was I thinking? I drop to my knees and wait for Skyler to find me – she'll track me pretty easily from the stream. Skyler and I had set rules in place, to ensure we'd be able to keep each other safe – and I'd just broken all of them.

Panic rises in me faster than the water in the stream, and before I know it I'm drowning. Skyler.

I need to get back to her, but in the excitement of the little girl appearing, I'm unsure of where I've just come from. I sniff the wind to see if I can catch her scent. But I smell something else. Blood.

It's quiet.

The kind of quiet that happens when every organism in the area knows what's good for them and gets out as quickly as they can. The recognition of the silence cuts into me, incapacitating me.

Danger is close.

I grasp for my knife and slowly rise from the ground. Eyes scanning the clearing, I stand, ready. Assessing the threat. Fight or flight. Live or die.

A branch snaps behind me. I whirl around. And just when I need to make the most important decision of my life, I freeze. Fear is a funny thing like that.

I hadn't planned on dying today.

1641

Skyler frowns. "A girl? You saw someone? A *child?*" She motions around her. "How had she survived until then? Who else is out there?"

"I don't know, Skyler," I admit. "I don't know."

FOUR

White Suit Man strolls nonchalantly into the room. I glare at him, but he doesn't seem particularly fazed by my anger. I can feel my rage radiate towards him but he just stares back placidly at me.

"Hello Ava."

I ignore the greeting.

"*Marked? Chosen?* I thought you meant everyone was Chosen. I mean, we all survived the Cull, didn't we? We've all been *chosen* to survive."

My gaze sears into White Suit Man. It is my turn to burn him now. He's all ice.

"Yes, Ava. Everyone is chosen to survive, but only a few can be elected, or Chosen, to lead. The Chosen are the new leaders of Haven. If leaders aren't selected it would be anarchy. Nothing good could come of that. You'll come to understand."

I want to believe this new world is a good thing, but I can't get over the idea of being Marked; of Skyler and I being tagged like animals.

He continues, "And of course, some must be chosen to guard you all, to keep the Marked – all of you – safe and sound. We call our soldiers and protectors of Haven, Guardians."

"And what if we don't want to stay? What if we want to look after ourselves? If we don't need Guardians to protect us," I retort.

"Don't want to stay? Skyler tells me you've been looking for somewhere like this. This is an *opportunity*, Ava. One you won't get again. When you're feeling better you can lead us to where your family is located and bring them here to you and to safety. Don't you want that?" He cocks his head to the side, like an animal that has clocked its prey. "All you have to do is agree to cooperate. To live by the standards as the Chosen see fit for your health."

I scowl over the idea of someone else looking out for my health, but he continues on.

"This includes regular testing and injections, to keep your immune system up. We don't want anyone to get sick. No more epidemics for us, or we'll be exterminated forever. The Marked's health and safety is our topmost priority. We are here to nurture. To protect. Haven is a good place. A safe place." He rattles off the information, glancing back at me frequently, eyes scanning over the entirety of my figure. Assessing the threat, I suppose. Or was it something else?

Either way, it unsettles me.

"Don't you want to be safe, Ava? He said we can stay here with other people, forever. They want to protect us, Ava." She is begging me with her eyes.

I feel sick again. Before I can reply, White Suit makes his way towards the door.

"Fantastic. It's settled then. Ava, you are very, *very* special to us. So, we want to see what you can do. We will give you your first round of injections shortly. You will stay here, until you are called later today. Apex, my personal Guardian will be here to assist you." He gestures to the burly man blocking the door. Apex glances toward me and I try not to shiver. There is a distance in those eyes as they assess me, a coldness.

"And Ava?"

I look up from Skyler's face to his.

"Leaving was never an option." He strides out of the room without a second glance. And that's when the nurse stabs me with the silver spear.

"What do you mean leaving – Argh!" I yell in pain. She does the same to Skyler, pushing the fluid held in the spear into our bodies.

The nurse looks utterly petrified as she does it. "Th—That was your first injection," she stammers. "You will receive them daily if you make it past the onboarding process. They will ensure you don't get sick." She shuffles off as two Guardians enter the room.

I grip the wall as my head spins. The world seems slow and blurry.

To ensure I don't get sick? This is the sickest I have felt in my entire life.

The noises beyond the room I could hear before are gone. I can't smell the scents of anyone in the room, like I could just moments ago. The details my vision could see before, that's gone too.

What is happening to me?

I grab Skyler's hand sloppily and pull her with me. We need to get away from these people. We need to run before it's too late. I go to punch the Guardian in my way but he blocks it with ease. My arms are so much slower, my body feels ... so much weaker.

The last thing I see is a fist coming toward my face.

CHAPTER

FIVE

They told me I'd be safe.

They told me my family would be looked after. They told me they wouldn't hurt us.

They lied.

Trust no one because trust gets you killed, or worse. That's what Mum had always said.

Well, I think I've found the meaning of worse.

SIX

The cell they've been keeping us in is so dark I can't even see my own hands in front of me. I hear Skyler crying in the corner of the room. It could have been days. It could have been months. I have no way to track the passing of time, no way to see the sun, or feel the breeze on my skin.

Is this what it feels like to die? Just an unending darkness stretching out for an eternity in front of you. We've had no food, no water. If they don't give us something fast, we'll be dead soon.

"Skyler..." I croak. But no response comes, just sniffles.

"Skyler you need to focus. When they open the door, we need to run."

"There's no point..." She mumbles weakly. "Didn't you see the fences as they lead us from the medical wing? That little spear they stabbed us with. It took our adapts. It weakened us. We can't fight like this. We'll be too slow if we run. They have guns. And too many Guardians. No point."

"Listen to me, Skyler, there is no way in hell I am going to let either one of us die like this. Soon our adapts will come back and then—"

Sunlight blinds me. It burns so much I cry out in pain. And then I hear that voice. The voice of the man who imprisoned us here. The voice of the man in a White Suit.

"Ava, Skyler. I see you have survived our onboarding process. Congratulations. Not everyone makes it this far."

I attempt to stand, to run. But the pain of the sunlight is too much. My legs won't do what they are told. Skyler was right. Our adapts are gone.

"Now, Ava. I have a little test for you. Something I have been thinking long and hard about. Guardians, you can take her. Skyler has no abilities out of the ordinary, nothing that hasn't been seen before. She can stay here for now."

"No—" I protest, but rough hands yank me to my feet and push me forward.

"Ava!" Skyler cries, but the door that has been trapping us slams shut, drowning her screams.

As my eyes adjust, I scan my surroundings. It's all grey, for miles around. Building upon building. They're identical. I can't even tell which one I've just come from.

Turn after turn, I am pushed and prodded. I make a wild attempt at a punch, so they restrain my hands. I try to scream for help, so they restrain my mouth. Another grey building, bigger than the rest, lies in front of me. From the little I can read, I can *just* make out the words 'Testing Centre' at its entrance.

White Suit walks a few metres ahead of me, not acknowledging my presence. I am pushed through the entrance, down a long hallway. In front of me, I see an iron door. White Suit opens it wide and gestures for me to enter: "Ladies first."

The room we walk into is indescribably huge. There are glass walls around us, trapping me in. I feel like I'm in one of those fish tanks Dad said he used to have before the Cull. From the darkness of the corners of the room emerge more white suits, more people that wear the same thing as the man before me. His scar glistens as he smiles at them. I notice that they do not enter into the fish tank with me, like White Suit and his Guardians have. They watch from afar. Women and men alike. Maybe twelve of them in all.

"Welcome, Chosen ones, the sons and daughters of Haven. I have a very exciting specimen to share with you. You all know what we face – a plight that does not need to be repeated with such receptive ears among us today." He gestures to me, and the Chosen chuckle along with him, like there's a joke I don't understand or something. Maybe I'm the punchline.

"We found one of the few free Marked left on this land. And she happens to be *extraordinary*." He draws that word out. "She may be able to help us." The Chosen's eyes seem to be alight with excitement, assessing me with something that looks like wonder.

"1641." He addresses me by the Mark he etched onto my unwilling skin. "Welcome to your first trial." He rips off the gag binding my mouth.

"If it means helping you in any way, how about I take that trial when *hell freezes over*." I spit.

"Oh, you won't be helping me. You'll be helping *him*. You may begin. Good luck. I hope you don't die, my dear. I have already grown so fond of your company."

At that precise moment, three things happen.

One: He stabs a small steel spear into my neck, pushing whatever is in it down into my bloodstream. I wince at the pain and then he and his Guardians are gone, a glass wall now separating me from them.

Two: A sound comes from above me. A trapdoor in the ceiling reveals a boy, who then proceeds to be pushed from the trapdoor onto the hard, cold floor I am standing on. He screams in pain as he tries to land on his feet, but his leg twists and he falls to the ground cradling it.

Three: The biggest Mute I've ever seen enters through a door that then snaps shut, leaving all three of us trapped together.

A loudspeaker echoes through the fish tank: "Ava, meet my favourite new pet, Goliath. He is so happy to meet you." Goliath looks anything but happy to meet me. He's what probably used to be a boar before the Cull, now ten times the size with hundreds of tusks all over his face and torso. He grinds a hoof slowly against the concrete floor; it screeches back in protest.

The boy – he must be around my age – looks at me in terror. From that look alone, I know he is not a fighter. I know he's not another predator the Chosen have trapped in the tank to fight it out. He's the prey. The reward the deadliest of us gets to claim. And that prey is either mine, or the Mute's.

"Get behind me," I instruct. He doesn't need to be told twice and limps toward me as fast as he can. My hands are still bound, but to my surprise I rip the silver bindings with ease. Energy and adrenaline pulses through every cell of my being.

The loudspeaker of White Suit's voice echoes again: "That injection I just administered causes a chemical reversal of the weakening serum. Your adapts are back, Ava. Show us what you can do with them."

"But I've got nothing to fight it with!" I protest, circling the Mute, never taking my eyes from it. It could attack at any second.

"Nonsense. I've given you the boy that you can lure it with, to distract it. If you give Goliath the boy, you can quite easily take him down while he is feasting. This Mute grows wild with the scent of blood."

A chill runs through me. He wants me to sacrifice this boy to survive. He's testing how far I'll go. How much I'm prepared to sacrifice in order to live.

The Mute lunges for me, and I grab the boy's arm and drag him with me. The Mute's tusks miss us by inches. "You're insane!" I yell at the glass wall. I hear the Chosen laugh at the panic in my voice.

"Can you fight?" I ask the boy behind me without turning around, ready and waiting for the next attack.

"N-No. I was my family's healer."

I roll my eyes. "Great."

Again, the Mute lunges at us. I propel myself off the glass wall with my foot and go to jump onto the Mute's back. The tusks are covering the front of its body, so its back is the weak spot I can use to take it down. I go to punch its back, but it feints to the side and I miss, rolling onto the concrete. I recover and jump to my feet, but I'm not fast enough. The Mute has already spotted the easiest prey. It stomps its hooves and breaks into a run toward the boy who is frozen in fear.

"Fall!" I yell at him.

"Wha —"

"Fall to the damn floor!" I scream. He drops to the floor on his stomach at the exact moment the tusks would have impaled him, if he'd still been standing. He lies still as the Mute charges over him. The Mute stills as it realizes his prey has outmanoeuvred him. In a second, I am by his side. The Mute rounds on us and lets out a scream of rage. I hear more laughter from outside the fish tank. Again, he charges.

Ava, this Mute is not intelligent. He just keeps going with the same tactics. I hear my Mother's voice in my mind.

If it's all brawn and no brains, I'm going to have to beat it with wits. *The Mute grows wild with the scent of blood.* That's what White Suit had said. "Argh!" Pain slices through my mouth. I bare my teeth at the

Chosen and they stop laughing. My adapts have kicked in. This time, in the form of razor-sharp teeth.

Seriously? I ask my body. *That's all you're giving me to fight this thing? I'm gonna bite it to death?*

As if in answer, I feel my fingernails sting. Tiny tusks have grown on them. I rip my fingernail – now a tusk – from my nail bed and grunt in pain. The boy's eyes widen in shock, but he says nothing.

"When I say so, you need to slice your hand open with this, ok? Make it bleed as much as you can." The boy nods solemnly. The Mute bursts into a gallop from the other side of the tank, roaring in fury. "Oh, and I'm going to throw you over the Mute," I add in quickly.

"What?!" He screeches. But I give him no time to argue, grabbing him by his shoulders. "Ow!" I loosen my grip as I see my claws are digging into him.

"You'll thank me later," I say, and I throw him in the opposite direction, flying over the top of the Mute and landing on the opposite side of the fish tank. As the Mute reaches me I yell, "Now!" The scent of blood floods the tank as the boy cuts his hand with my tusk.

The Mute pauses its attack and turns towards the scent of the boy's blood. It's just for a moment, but a moment's all I need. I slide underneath the Mute's body. My claws slice its belly open and blood gushes down onto me. The Mute screams as I fish inside its body, feeling for what I need. I rip out its heart with one vicious tug. It falls on top of me and is still.

A stunned silence is all that greets my victory. Followed by a slow clap. I push the Mute off me, discarding the heart as quickly as I'd found it.

"How marvellous! You truly are something else, 1641. You have passed your first trial. Your reward is the boy's life. We need to subdue you, however – and get that weakening serum back in your system, so you can't do any damage to my Guardians, apologies for this." A smoke descends from the trapdoor the boy had emerged from, just minutes ago.

The boy tries to help me up, offering me his hand.

"I hardly need your help," I growl. "I saved your ass just a second ago, remember?"

"Thank you," is all he says. The smoke is circling us now, I breathe it in, suddenly drowsy. I would like to go to sleep. Yes, sleep is what I need...

"You're welcome," I slur, before the darkness takes me.

SEVEN

I don't recognize the face in front of me as I wake. And then the horrors of this morning come flooding back to me. The boy I'd saved. It's him, right there in front of me. I try to sit up. *I need to find Skyler.* My breathing becomes rapid as I think about what they might have done to her while I've been in the fish tank.

"Hey, easy," he says. "Your body will be adapting to the serum injection the Doctor just administered."

Serum injection?

"You mean – the venom, the steel spear? They are called injections?"

"Yeah. And they're a bitch alright. If we didn't have *that* permanently in our systems, my guess is we could give these fences keeping us locked in here a run for their money."

I assess the room I now find myself in. No one else seems to be around, but beds stretch across the entirety of the space. They are all stacked up on top of each other, in four vertical rows. The space between each of them is so small there's barely enough room to lie down on one. The room is filthy. Even with the serum back in my system, and without my stronger senses, it stinks.

"Skyler..." I say and try to sit up again.

"Your friend? She will be out with the rest of the women assigned to this room. She'll be working."

"Working?" I frown.

"If you refuse to work for them, you die. It's mostly labour, to build more places they can keep us locked in, ironically enough. But if you stop working even for a second, they execute you."

"I have to..." I try and sit up again, but my head is spinning.

"Whoa, easy. I've been told to keep you here for the rest of the day. To heal you. Healing is kind of my thing, like I said ... when we met." He swallows and his eyes seem to drift away from the present moment, probably reliving the nightmare of our earlier encounter. Now the adrenaline from almost being mauled by that Mute has worn off, I can pay attention to what I see in front of me.

The boy's face is pale and drawn, no doubt due to the starvation and beatings, but I can still recognize a certain handsomeness in him: high cheekbones, full lips, a gap just slightly too large between his front two teeth as he smiles at me tentatively. He has dark features, his eyes, hair and skin all a beautiful shade of dark brown.

"I'm Kai." He tilts his head, examining me.

"Ava."

"It's an honour to meet the famous Ava." He bows mockingly, imitating the voice of the man who had almost killed us both. For the first time in days, I smile. It's small and it's slow but it's there. He continues, "Ok, no seriously. What you did back there? That was *crazy*. I have never seen anything like that on the outside, let alone in Haven. I mean, I've seen some humans that have developed specific adaptations relative to the environment or their genes, but it's always minor stuff. Maybe being able to see in the dark, or I don't know, the ability to be underwater for a significant portion of time but that..." His eyes are assessing me. I shift uncomfortably. "You can..."

"...literally adapt to my environment, as I encounter it, yeah."

"Ava, that's like – no one can do that."

"Yeah, well, I can't either now," I sigh. I try to get up, but my body is too weak. I can feel my adapts are gone. "They've injected me with that stuff again."

"Yeah, but even without your adapts, I bet you can still fight pretty damn well. You need to teach me how to fight like that." I shift in my bed. He shakes his head, a sudden tentativeness in his eyes. "Sorry. I know you must be tired but um, I need to see your hand again. To check if it needs more salve."

"My hand?" As I say it, I notice an immense pain in my finger. I lift it to assess the damage. Maybe it's broken.

But it's not there.

I forget how to breathe.

"Wh—what the...?!" I scream. The top half of my finger is *gone*. Usually, if I'm hurt, things regenerate, but with the serum in my body stopping me from using my adapts...

"Hey, whoa. Calm down please, Ava. *Please* Ava, if you scream they will come in here and take me away, and I won't be able to heal you."

"Heal me?! You're gonna magically heal my finger back onto my hand?! What the hell happened to me, Kai?!"

"The Doctor. The one in the white suit. When you passed out from the smoke. He wanted samples of you. Your genetic makeup. What he wants with them, I don't know. He took your hair, and he wanted your blood, bone, skin and an example of your adapts. Your fingers still had those tusk things on them. So he ... took one. I'm so sorry, Ava. I'm trying to decrease the damage he's done as much as possible, so when you get your adapts back, your body can heal and it might grow back."

"Might?!"

"I'm so sorry. There's nothing else I can do. I know, you saved my life. It feels pathetic that I can't do more for you." He scowls and I see that the fact he can't help me pains him. He *wants* to help me. God knows why. I'm a freak. A literal genetic freak. When I learned what my body could do, how different I was, Mum had always told me to hide it. That people would want my gifts and try to take them for themselves. Or in this case, take my *body parts* for themselves. I feel sick.

"It's ok, Kai." I say as I swallow down the pain. "Just do what you can."

I don't talk much after that, but he chatters on about his life before Haven, about his mother and how she taught him the science and art of healing. He is from the indigenous people of this land, the Māori, he tells me. He is relentless in his talking, making jokes and telling stories, despite this awful place we are in. He's so animated it's hard not to be pulled into them. I feel the dull ache in my finger disappearing.

"Where the hell have you been?!" Skyler screeches as she bursts into the room, heading straight for where I lie, still too weak to get up.

"It's a long story and it's resulted in minus one finger so I'd rather not talk about it,"

Kai gets up from his perch on my bed, Skyler practically shoving him off to take his place. She assesses my hand with horror. "And who's this?" She inclines her head towards Kai before raking her eyes across the rest of my body, checking for injuries.

"I'm Kai." He throws a radiant smile and a hand out towards her.

She looks at him in disgust. "And what's that for?" she says, gesturing at his hand.

"It's ... for a handshake. They used to do it before the Cull..." He looks around awkwardly and drops the hand quickly. "Well, um, nice to meet you, Skyler. I'll see you soon, Ava. And thank you. For you know, not using my blood as bait and saving my life and all."

Kai turns away and limps out of the room, no doubt from his fall earlier. He dodges past the rest of the Marked women who have now made their way in from a long day of gruelling work. I suddenly feel guilty. He'd spent all afternoon looking after me, when he'd no doubt been in pain, and needed to see a healer himself. The other Marked women throw me distrustful looks, but most just ignore me and head straight for their beds, too exhausted to notice someone new in their midst.

"I'm gonna kill that bastard," Skyler growls.

"Skyler. He tested me. He took samples." I lift my hand and wince in pain. "Whatever I am, whatever I can do, he wants to know how I can do it. For some reason, I'm useful to him."

Skyler shakes her head in worry. "Can no one else here do what you can? We always wondered if there would be more like you out there. Is there no one else?"

"I don't think so. Which means we have a target on our backs. We need to figure out how we are going to get out of here Skyler, and fast."

EIGHT

He laughs as I fall to the floor.

"You're really quite stubborn, aren't you? Carry on, Apex. Make sure you don't damage her face."

My stomach explodes with agony as Apex's foot connects. I curl into a ball, attempting to protect myself with the little strength I have left. I wish I could fight back, but my body won't let me.

Skyler's screams push through the wall. She is in the room next door and completely out of reach.

They are looking for information today.

I hope with every part of my being that she doesn't tell them where my family is. I don't know what I'd do if the Chosen found them too. If they were doing this to me and I was special ... someone they wanted alive ... then I'd shudder to think of what they'd do to Xander. Or Dad.

I slump to the floor. The fragility of my body is astounding. I am all bones. Splintering and cracking and breaking. It feels as if I'm going to snap at any moment.

White Suit sighs. "Let's come back tomorrow, Apex. I'm tired." I see him smooth out his suit jacket. "Let her think about what has been said."

He slowly makes his way towards me. I cower in the corner, my face turned away from his. I hate that I cannot fight back, that I can't protect myself. That I'm reduced to this. Nothing more than a hopeless piece of prey caught in a predator's trap.

I choke back the stinging sensation in my eyes and eventually find the courage to turn and look at him with as much hate as I can muster.

"Now, 1641." His lips curl up into a smile, but his eyes are devoid of all feeling, all empathy. How had I not noticed the cruelty in those black eyes? I wish I'd run that day. I wish I'd taken Skyler and run.

But it's too late.

"You are proving to be a difficult test subject. Not only do you refuse to tell me anything of any use to Haven, or the whereabouts of your family, but you continue to disobey orders when put to work by my Guardians. You are becoming extremely difficult to tame. The outside world has made you simply feral. Thank goodness we found you when we did."

He draws even closer to me. He exhales, his hot breath too close to my face. "No matter, I will break you. Even if I have to do it myself." He drags a finger down the right side of my face delicately, forehead to chin, almost as if mimicking the pattern of the scar on his own. He pauses, his fingers on my cheek.

"My. Name. Is. Ava."

Courage or stupidity overcomes me. I don't know which, a bit of both maybe. I spit in his face. He rises slowly, dabbing his scar with a crimson silk cloth he has produced from his pocket – but I catch the look of anger, even hurt on his face.

I stare back at him defiantly. *I'm not planning on letting you break me anytime soon.*

He senses my message before nodding to Apex, and I get a punch in the jaw as a thank you. I fall once again, my ears ringing.

This time I don't get up. White Suit Man calls outside the dark cell.

"Guardian Ryder – take 1641 back to her cell but clean her up first. I want her fresh for interrogation tomorrow morning."

And then he's gone.

Ryder? He never addresses Guardians by name.

I hear the echo of heavy footsteps. A Guardian is supposed to protect the Marked in Haven. Their job is to keep us 'safe and happy' in this new Utopia, as I've heard White Suit Man say. He explains it to the Marked in his daily brainwashing, mind-numbing speeches about how the Marked should feel lucky to be here, in the promised land of Haven. That we are safe from the outside world that so nearly destroyed us all. But we all know they are empty words.

I'd rather face a hundred Mutes and be free than be in Haven right now.

I tense my abdomen, ready for more impact, yet another kick or punch, but nothing happens.

Instead I am lifted into the air by the Guardian. I flinch in surprise. Every touch I have received from a Guardian has caused only agony. My attempts to push him away are futile and his arms pull me closer to his chest to restrain my movements. I can feel the power in them. I try to pull myself from his grip again. But he says calmly,

"It's ok. I'm not going to hurt you."

This small indication of some sort of humanity unlocks something deep inside of me.

I am unravelled.

For four days, I've been living in horror, living in fear of death and pain. How could he make such a promise, when he knows he can't keep it? Eventually he would have to hurt me. I do not look at him as I let the tears spill out. He says nothing; he just keeps walking. My tears run on and on.

I wipe the tears away with the back of my shaking hand. We walk past a sign that reads 'Medical Wing' and I think of the books Mum made me read about something they had before the Cull: hospitals. Doctors and nurses used to help people there. These days, they just seem to test and torture people. I wonder how such a caring profession had resulted in a doctor like White Suit Man, so brutal, so cruel.

The Guardian sets me down on a steel table and begins his work, locating the correct materials to clean me up. He puts some water on my face before opening up a small glass bottle – it smells odd. The harsh scent, even with my weakened senses makes me blink in surprise.

It stings as he applies it. It's burning me. "Ah..." I hiss, my hand shooting toward the pain. It feels sticky. I remove my hand and examine the blood running across my fingers.

"Don't touch it," he commands. "It's called disinfectant. It will stop your injury from getting infected, and you getting sick. Your body can't heal as quickly as it used to. You could get a fever."

I say nothing in return, staring at the ground. I refuse to look at him. He said he wouldn't hurt me. He already has. He reaches towards me with something in his hand and I jump back off the bed. He is holding see-through rocks; they drip as he looks at me in confusion.

"Ice." He nods at the rocks in his hands. "It will help with the swelling. Sit down."

As he puts the ice on my cheek, where Apex's final punch landed, I scowl at the pain but do not move away from him. My lowered eyes travel up and peer into his square face. As he holds the ice there, focused on my cheek, there is an intensity to his honey-brown eyes. Dark stubble etches his jawline. He looks young. He can't be more than a few years older than me.

The silence is deafening. I just want to go back to my cell. To find Skyler and hug her. To find Kai and see if he is ok. His gaze never breaks from the task at hand: my cheek. His intensity is unsettling. I can't help but become curious about this strange boy helping me.

No, helping *them*.

"You get used to it, you know."

I ignore his attempt at a conversation. I drop my eyes to the ground yet again and stay quiet. He waits for my response and realizes it's not coming, so he continues.

"The injections that are making you feel like you can't stand up or move well. I had that. The weakening serum, it takes a lot out of you. All of your strength, your speed. I mean, my strength isn't what it was once, but I guess I'm equivalent to a normal human being now, before the Cull happened. They still make me take a small amount of the serum – that was part of the deal."

I don't understand until he turns around. A small mark tattooed on the back of his neck: 1000. "You're Marked?" I stutter, "Why would you help *them*? Why would you help the Chosen keep us here? They are *killing* people. They are torturing us."

I wrench myself away from his grasp, stumbling a little as I stand. "Stay the hell away from me," I warn. "I don't care if you were supposed to heal me. My name is not 1641 – it's Ava. Get *away* from me."

I give him one final shove before I start to descend into dizziness. I fall from the sudden exertion, nausea gripping me in its tight clasp, but the Guardian's quick reflexes catch me, and he steadies me on my feet. I snarl at him and he quickly removes his hands from my shoulders. He looks taken aback by my snarl, almost afraid of me. Good.

His jaw tightens, and his eyes become steel. I find myself wanting to sink away at the coldness in his face, but I hold the stare. *Never let your opponent see you weak.* My mother's voice echoes in my mind. "If anyone else heard you say that, you could be executed." I find myself wondering how he was able to turn so quickly. That warm intensity I saw just a moment ago has become cold and distant. "Speaking ill of Haven is treason, punishable by death.

He looks up and subtly signals to a small camera in the room. "The security cameras can't pick up sound, just movement – and it's bad quality. That's as good as they've been able to get it after the Cull. But I need to shove you back so we don't look suspicious. Alright?"

I nod slowly.

He takes me in his grip and does just that, but holds the back of my head as he does it, to not jolt my neck from the impact.

"Why don't you, then?" I demand.

"Why don't I what?" he asks.

"Execute me." I swallow.

"I respect bravery." I turn away before he can say anything else. He doesn't make any sense. He's supposed to be my enemy. He's supposed to hurt me. "The Doctor let you keep your hair?"

I've come to realize it's protocol for Marked to have their hair shaved off. Mine is the only head of hair in Haven's hundreds of Marked. It gets me a lot of untrusting stares from the other Marked.

"He says I can keep it because I'm of use to him. He says it's a gift," I say carefully.

"I see." His eyes stay neutral. I avoid them at all costs.

"I won't be having it for long," I say as I grimace. "I pissed him off today. He said if I can keep it only if I decide to cooperate."

"And what did you say?" He seems to know already.

"I told him where to shove it."

I see a ghost of a smile play on his lips, but then it's gone and I wonder if I've seen it all. I see how he's careful not to let the camera see his subtle movements, turning away from it when he speaks to me.

The siren sounds, making me jump. The siren marks the end of another day of hard and exhausting labour for the Marked. At the sound, Guardians escort all the Marked back to their cells. If they are lucky they might get a meal before the routine of being worked to death starts all over again tomorrow.

I dodge out of his way and slowly begin to limp out of the room. I'm careful not to look too hard at him or act too casually in case the cameras see. I should be afraid of him. I don't know why I'm not.

"1641?"

I turn at the sound of my number. Now that I'm standing, I have a different view of the Guardian. He is taller than me, just a little.

When he speaks, his voice is soft but firm. "Try not to get yourself killed."

NINE

Our stomachs are full of fish and a five-legged rabbit we caught on the way home. I mentally thank whoever or whatever's up there that we are still lucky enough to have animals that survived the Cull that aren't as dangerous as the Mutes. I try not to think about the ones that hunt us. But it's hard to put them out of my mind, when we come face to face. Or face to ... snout. Whatever. I'm not going down without a fight either way.

I turn my attention towards Dad as he looks vacantly out of the cave into the dark sky of stars in front of us. Our home is perfect. A huge chasm a few hundred metres up a cliff. I can hunt knowing they're safe, and we can sleep without having anyone on watch for Mutes. It wasn't an easy task getting our belongings up here, but we managed it. Rock climbing up and down the steep cliff, hauling my Dad on my back to get to this place was definitely not a task I'd like to repeat again anytime soon. It was worth the *effort though. When you've got height, protection and invisibility, you've got the upper hand. We've been up here since Mum died. When we lost her, we had to move on – we had to find somewhere safe. And this was the best option I'd seen for us since … well, since then.*

He breaks the comfortable silence we've been sitting in. He speaks slowly, hesitantly, as if this has been on his mind for a while. "Since the … attack, you've been carrying a burden. I'm glad Skyler's here to help you. Thank you, Ava. You've kept us alive this long. I have faith you'll continue to." He pulls me into his side and I smile in the embrace.

1 6 4 1

"Ava? Ava!" Xander calls from across the cave, the sound echoing around the dark hall. "Can you read me a story before bed?"

Skyler ruffles his dark hair, feigning mock horror. "What's wrong with me, huh?" she asks.

"I want Ava," Xander pouts. I suppress a smile.

Closing the gap between us, I take him into my arms, pulling him into a big bear hug. "Alright, Xanny, get into bed and I will." I slip into the sleeping bag beside Xander. His ice-blue eyes gaze expectantly into my own, his eyebrows raised slightly in anticipation. My smile grows as he wriggles closer and I begin.

1 6 4 1

"Mum, why do I have to do drills when none of the other kids do?" I moan.

"Just because there hasn't been a Mute attack on this settlement for over a year, doesn't mean there never will be. The defences are good, yes, but you never know. If the other parents don't want me to train their kids, fine. But

I'll be damned if I let you grow up not knowing how to defend yourself."
Her voice is hard. It is not up for discussion.

"Positions!" She calls. I throw up my sparring knives with a sigh. I
glance toward the ten other children of the settlement playing for just a
second, before she attacks.

1 6 4 1

Screams. Blood. That is all I can see and hear as Mum drags me from the
tent. Xander, just a baby in her arms. I am shaking and crying. I don't
understand how this Mute has found us. We had been safe for so long.

My eyes widen as I see Dad fighting the Mute, with only knives to pro-
tect him against those massive claws.

Mum hands Xander to me. "Ava. Listen to me. Your dad and I are the
only ones trained enough to take it down. You need to take Xander and
run. We need to buy everyone else who survived some time. We'll be right
behind you. Climb up the highest tree you can find and wait there until
you see Dad or I, ok?"

"But Mum, you've trained me. I can help." My hands shake at the offer
I have just made, but my gaze stays true.

"No. You need to look after Xander. That is your job now. Your most
important job. To protect. Do you understand me?"

"Yes, Mum."

"Now go."

I run and run and I don't look back.

1 6 4 1

"Ava. *Ava.* Wake up. It's ok. *Wake up.*" Skyler pushes my hair back from
my sticky forehead. Tears streak my cheeks.

"It was a dream ... but it wasn't. My memories," I whisper to her. "Dad and Xander. They are all I dream about now. We won't ever see them again. How are they going to eat? Who's going to protect them?"

I will never again brush away the salty tears painted on my brother's face from his nightmares. I will never see him grow into a man. And it's all my fault. When I ran after that girl I killed us all.

We are interrupted by the sound of men shouting. Guardians throw open our cell door and yell, "Out!" at the women sleeping around me.

They force us out of the cramped and dirty rooms to wash ourselves under something called a shower. It spits at me spitefully as I duck in and then out of the icy water droplets. We only have a few seconds to wash the stench from ourselves. Having to dry naturally, and only being given rags to wear, we would get sick if we were under the cold water for any longer. And if you are too sick to work, you're dead.

Hundreds of women, men, and children scramble and fight their way through the throngs to get to the front of the line, for just a few seconds to wash. As I make a beeline to the back of the pushing crowd I see a woman ask a Guardian if they are allowed food today. He responds by slapping her to the floor.

"Ava?" I know that voice. Kai.

"Hey," I whisper back. We hide behind a group of men waiting in line for the showers, out of the Guardians' view. They are posted everywhere – and they all have those damn guns.

I had been excited about finding a gun before; it could have been a way to protect my family against Mutes.

Now the very idea of a gun terrifies me.

I inch towards Kai. "You got any of the...?"

"Oh, so that's how it's going to be, huh? You gonna use me for my connections?" Kai teases, with mock horror playing on his features.

"Well, I guess you did save my life and all, so..." His dark brown eyes sparkle as he hands me the bread he's stolen.

I devour it in seconds, saving half for Skyler for when I find her again, hiding it in my grey cotton rags, the trademark Marked uniform. It's barely enough to keep us decently covered, let alone find a place to hide bread, but I manage to tuck it away safely from view.

"You're such an asshole," I mumble in-between my hurried bites, stealing furtive looks around me to make sure no one is watching us. Besides the injections, the measly food rations keep us weak. By now, we are probably even weaker than those humans who lived before the Cull twenty years ago, before any adapts. I feel sorry for them and the poor strength they had to endure. How did they survive like this? I can barely move some days. My bones feel brittle and weak and one punch leaves me with purple and yellow splotches all over my skin.

I look out expectantly towards the fence that holds us in its grasp. Kai follows my gaze and tells me what I already know: "Electric," Kai says. "If you touch it when you're like this, it'd be immediate death."

"I know," I admit.

Haven is large, with hundreds of Marked, Guardians, and Chosen alike. Every time I see those huge fences, the barriers keeping us from our freedom, I feel as if I might suffocate. Its grey buildings stretch on forever – grey block of cells, after grey block of cells. I get lost constantly because everywhere you turn it looks the same. What I wouldn't give to see a bit of green somewhere. Not even the centre of Haven has anything remotely close to nature. It's pure concrete. Every single wall. I see only in monochromatic now, the white of the Chosen as they scuttle through Haven protected by the black Guardian uniforms, and the grey box of a world I am now living in. If only I was as strong as I was before, I could scale those barriers with ease. Never mind the electricity – I could endure it. Never mind the bullets that I'm sure would be flying at my head – I could dodge them.

These days? There's no chance. No chance of escape, no chance of freedom. "Do you ever miss it?" I ask.

"Miss what? Not almost dying on a daily basis?" Sarcasm drips in Kai's voice as he breathes the cold mist out from his mouth onto his hands, rubbing them together.

"That, yeah." I give him a sideways glance. "And the ... power ... you know, before the injections. We were so much more than what humans used to be twenty years ago. We could do anything. We were so strong, so fast. I was so scared on the outside all the time. Now I just wish I'd taken a couple more chances."

The crowd moves forward slightly and a man shoves me, trying to get to the water. I shove back. I know Kai won't do it. He's too kind, too gentle, so I do it on his behalf most of the time. You've got to stay tough in here or more than just Guardians will take advantage of your weakness. The man gives me a glare and I glare right back.

"Well with what you've got going on in that body of yours, you definitely could have taken some wild chances out there." He smirks but then his eyes grow sombre as he answers my question: "All the time. But you know what? One day, we're going to get it back. Our strength, our speed, everything. And we'll see how the Chosen and Guardians like it then." Kai's gravelly voice has become intense, his face hard, his jaw tight. "I'm going to get out of here. Very soon." He seems like he wants to say more but stops himself as his eyes fix on a point behind me.

"The Doctor wishes to see you." I recognize the voice, so I put on my best glare of hatred and turn to inspect Guardian Ryder coolly. His gaze is cold and clinical: he's in Guardian mode today. The softness I saw in him on that first day, the mercy, it's gone. He has Skyler next to him, a gun pressed into her small frame; a small reminder that this isn't a request, it's an order. She has her head hung low, but her eyes dart to mine for a second; we don't need to speak for me to know she's been doing something she shouldn't have. I hope she isn't going to get us killed before the week is out. I want to cause a little more damage before I go.

"Both of us?" I ask. The waver in my voice betrays me. What if he wants me to do another trial, like last time?

"Yes." He glances over to Kai, steely as ever, and Kai returns Ryder's glare tenfold. I realize I'm grateful to have him by my side. Kai squeezes my hand, one eyebrow up, almost testing Ryder's patience, seeing how far he can push it.

"See you later, ok?" Kai confirms. I nod slowly, to both Ryder's request and Kai's expectation.

Ryder has already begun walking up the gravelled steps towards the Doctor's office, gun still pressed into Skyler. I follow reluctantly. I let him lead the way through the throngs of Marked, setting out towards their duties for the day, eyes cast down. My feet lead me to where I am meant to go, and I trudge up the cobbled steps to the main building where the Doctor's offices are, trailing a little behind Ryder.

We walk towards the largest building, just behind the town square. A sign reads: '*Chosen Quarters. Marked are forbidden past this point unless accompanied.*' There is another post of Guardians outside several more doors along the building. Ryder produces something that reads 'Identification Card' and he is waved through.

Ryder places black bindings our wrists. I scowl at the scratchy material and the fact that strangulation is no longer an option for me to kill White Suit Man. His calloused hand brushes mine as he works and I rip my bound wrists away from him, a low growl of warning in my throat. His eyes meet mine and I see something in them that almost looks wounded at my aggression. His jaw tenses and he jerks his chin towards something I have learnt is called a door. Doors can shut and lock you in, if they want to. Just like fences. And walls. I have decided I hate doors.

I grind my teeth in anticipation of seeing the Doctor's grotesque face. My stomach aches with hunger and I am shaking from the cold morning but my mind is focused. It's focused on one thing, and one thing only. *What can I use in here to kill White Suit?*

TEN

"Ava and Skyler. My two savage girls."

The Doctor gestures to the seats in front of us and Skyler and I exchange a worried glance. What cruelty has he got planned for us today? We begin to make our way to the seats in front of his desk, and I glance at Ryder who is standing in the doorway. His back is to us, surveying the rest of Haven. He probably knows we aren't even enough of a threat to be watched, bound like this.

"Now, I'm sorry for the unpleasantness of your first few days here," he says, with a voice as smooth as silk. "I believe we got off on the wrong foot. All that nasty business. I really didn't want to have to do that, but I needed to know where your family resides, so I can bring them here and keep them safe."

Yeah, right. You keeping my family safe is about as likely as a Mute telling me a bedtime story.

He continues, "And any others that may be with them." His onyx eyes stare expectantly into my own, waiting for my response.

"Skyler and I have told you. We know nothing of a larger group. It's just our family. That's it."

White Suit operates under the deluded theory that I am a part of a larger community determined to take Haven down. Through various interrogations and beatings, I've figured out he believes that finding my family's location is the key to finding the rest of a Resistance movement. He goes on and on with questions about this so-called Resistance – where they hide out, when they plan to invade Haven, how many are in their army.

"I guess you'll have to see for yourself when your Guardians find them, that it's just my family, no Resistance, no secret group trying to burn down this shit hole." I say through gritted teeth.

"Ava," Skyler warns, but the Doctor just grins back at me never releasing me from his gaze.

"Burn, you say? Interesting."

"She didn't mean – it was just a figure of speech. She has no idea where these people are, Doctor. They don't exist. We've told you that. And when you find Ava's family, you'll know we are telling the truth," Skyler says. She glances towards the door and shifts uncomfortably in her seat. She knows I lied to him. I made up a location and told him my family was there.

I'd never give them up. I'd die before I'd betray them to him. With any luck, they'll be on a wild-goose chase for at least a week. But when the Guardians return and inform White Suit that I lied about their location, I'm dead – or worse.

"Yes, well, we will just have to wait and see until the Guardians return with your family and whomever else your group is harbouring, won't we?" He rises from his chair and makes his way over to my seat, standing right in front of me, his face tilted towards my own. "I'm so excited to have them all here with us."

I gulp at the thought.

"You wouldn't lie to me, would you, Ava?" He strokes my hair. I calmly resist the urge to bite his finger off. That probably won't do me any favours at this present moment.

"I'm glad I let you keep this," he says as fingers trace their way down my scalp. "The length suits you." His hand drifts past my neck to my collarbone, not touching me, but close enough to make me shiver. I seethe in silence.

"Don't you think, Ryder?" His cold eyes turn to Ryder behind me.

"S- Sorry, Sir?" he stutters, whirling around. This is the first time I've seen Ryder look nervous, even slightly afraid.

"Don't you think Ava's hair looks lovely like this?" He is a frozen statue waiting for Ryder's response.

"Y—Yes, Sir, I do."

"It reminds me of someone, you know."

Ryder's eyes dart from White Suit to me and back. "Yes, Sir?"

White Suit rolls his eyes and looks back at me, giving me a wink. He looks slightly deranged. "Brothers are such strange things aren't they?"

"Ryder's not my brother," I mumble. Ryder is frozen to the spot.

"Oh, I know that." His eyes are no longer far away, dark and cruel, they stare into my own. "I wasn't talking about him. I was talking about the wonderful Xander. I simply can't wait to meet him."

I feel like a mouse being tossed in each paw. He is playing with his food before he eats it, savouring every terrified squeak I make. I resolve to not give him the satisfaction and simply stare back at him.

Skyler's breathing gets harder and more audible. She knows we are in danger, but this time it isn't like dealing with a Mute. No, Mutes will attack you outright. This species, this hateful kind that he belongs to, seem to prefer much subtler tactics.

"No," I say. "I would never lie to you."

"No, what?"

I swallow the bile that begs to be released. "No ... Sir."

"Good. Your samples from your first task have yielded very positive results. I wish to keep you comfortable, until the time is right." I grind my teeth, and force myself not to look to the state my finger is in. What he took from me. Kai has been trying as hard as he can, but with the serum in my body, it hasn't grown back.

"Until the time is right for what?" I ask.

He doesn't answer for a moment. He likes drawing these moments out, I can tell. "You'll see."

I gulp. What if he knows my secret already? What if he already knows I've sent his Guardians the wrong direction, away from my family and not towards them? For now, he doesn't seem to let on anything if he does. I suck in air and hold it. I bite my tongue hard until I taste blood.

"You're a special girl, Ava, and your results have confirmed that. Such a special little girl..." He mutters, turning away. With his back towards us he looks out the window towards his Haven, the grey cage he has created stretching out below us.

"I think it's about time you had a new task, don't you?"

ELEVEN

The fish tank looks the same way I'd left it. Sterile. Unfeeling.

White Suit had forced Skyler to come with us. He pulls her next to him, her hands still bound in a way that makes me want to bite *his* stupid hand off. Her breath is rapid as she looks around the other Chosen that have all gathered to watch my trial from outside the fish tank. All in white, they examine her with interest and disgust simultaneously.

White Suit motions and the door to the fish tank opens, and Ryder leads me inside. The loudspeaker in the tank echoes so loudly I flinch in discomfort. "Ava. I am *so* very thrilled to have you with us again to-day," he says, as if I'd just agreed to be the guest of honour at his party, rather than locked up against my will and tested like an animal. "Aren't we all thrilled?" I hear the other Chosen murmur in assent over the loudspeaker, all looking absolutely fascinated. Ryder shifts uncomfort-ably next to me, as if he's unsure what's to come too.

"Ryder," White Suit commands, "you may inject the subject with the antidote and make your way out of the testing lab."

Ryder looks to me, his face contorted in an expression that looks a little bit like worry. But it can't be. He's a monster, just like the rest of them. "I'm sorry," he says, and then there's a stab in my neck. Like before, my knees buckle from the impact of the injection.

But unlike before, I know what to do this time.

I lunge for Ryder. I rip the gun from his holster on his leg and aim it at him. He holds his hands up in mercy. "Let me out," I say to the Doctor. "Let Skyler go, or I'll kill him."

"By all means my dear, be my guest. There's plenty more Guardians around. One less is no burden to me." The gun I have pointed toward Ryder starts to shake as White Suit continues: "Go on, then. Kill him and be done with it. I want to start the trial." He sounds like a pouting child. I change tack.

Leaping toward Ryder, I hold him in front of me as a shield and begin shooting at the glass that separates me in the testing room from Skyler, White Suit and the other Chosen. Bullets fly, but the glass does not even shudder at the impact. I run forward and kick it, punch it. With my strength back to normal, surely it would move. And once I got out of here, at full strength, we could get away. I scream in indignation as the glass wall in front of me holds steady. The other Chosen begin jotting down notes intently, as if I was some sort of case study, which enrages me all the more. I scream as my dream of freedom seeps away in front of me. Unless...

White Suit is directly in front of me now, the unbreakable glass the only thing between us. I look him directly in the eye and lift the gun to my own head. His expression morphs from panic, to grief, to rage. "You wouldn't." he hisses.

"Try me, asshole."

In an instant, he has Skyler – next to him only seconds ago – on the floor. He's choking her. Skyler claws at his hands, her eyes wide in terror but he does not move. "If you die, she dies. And slowly. And, to throw in a little bonus, if you pull that trigger 1641, I'll kill every Marked child in here. And that healer boy you've grown so fond of."

I drop the gun from its position at my head as quickly as I'd taken it. He smiles and releases Skyler, and she scrambles up to stand, coughing and rubbing her neck. There are already bruises there. "Good girl. Now give the gun to Guardian Ryder," he says in a monotonous voice, "and then we'll get on with the trial. Do not disobey me again." His voice is cold and quiet. I throw the gun to Ryder, his expression is unreadable as he leaves the tank, shutting and locking the entrance. "1641, you may begin. You have five minutes on the clock. You need to keep them alive until then. Try and use your adapts to do so."

"Them? Who's..." I say. But before I can finish, the trapdoor Kai fell through opens, and a woman with her child are lowered down to the room, a rope tying them to eachother and suspending them from the ceiling of the fish tank, their hands bound. The woman is trying to comfort the crying child, who looks about the same age as Xander.

With a hiss, water begins to rush in from three other trap doors in the floor, and the fish tank begins to fill. In a few seconds it's already up to my waist. *Shit.* "Alright, stay there, and stay calm. Panicking will only make it worse, ok?" I say to them. Both the woman and child nod solemnly. They are still suspended by a rope, their current height at about the middle of the fish tank. With the water rising at this rate, I need to get them as high as possible, and fast.

I swim to the side of the tank and begin to attempt to climb up the side of the glass, but my hands slip. There is nothing for me to grab onto, so I can climb up the wall, like the rocks on the cliffs at home. And then the palms of my hands become sticky. *Really* sticky. My adapts must be back. I begin to climb up the glass, the water still churning and rising beneath me. I reach the top of the tank, right by the trap door, and use one hand to keep myself suspended on the roof of the tank, and the other to pull the rope up toward me. The water is already at their feet by the time I reach them. "I've got to keep you both attached to this rope, ok? I can't hold onto both of you and keep us up this high."

"Please, whatever happens. Save her. Save my girl. That has to be your priority. Swear to me?" Her eyes are hard and unafraid. I think of my mother and the day she chose my life over her own. I think of Xander and Skyler and what I would want if the tables were turned. I nod. The water has already risen too high. I start to slam the top of the trap door, to see if there's a way through, but it's immovable. "Damn it," I swear. "It's not moving. There's no way out."

"It's ok," the woman comforts her child. "This girl is going to save you. You're going to live." I can't help but feel as if this sounds like a goodbye. Now, we are all treading water, the water level about to rise above our heads any second now.

"Argh!" I scream. An intense pain like nothing I've felt before hits me. I reach my hand to the point of the pain on my neck. I can feel three tiny slits in my skin. The woman looks at me and gasps.

"Gills."

All three of our heads go underwater at the same time. "Save her!" I hear the mother scream underwater. I motion for her to save her energy, save her breath as I take the child's hand. I close my eyes. I focus every piece of feeling and energy I have on this child. It's up to me to save her. And I will not fail.

The last thing I see before I black out is a little girl staring back at me, with a small pair of gills of her own.

I wake on the floor of the fish tank, soaked through. Skyler and Ryder are both in there with me. The Chosen and White Suit are gone.

"Wh—what happened?"

"You were incredible." Skyler rushes toward me, helping me up and taking my hand. Ryder makes no such move but simply stares out of the fish tank, as if he were locked in here himself.

"Skyler," I pant. "What happened?"

"You... White Suit said his hypothesis was right. Your adapts can be pushed from yourself to another in a life-threatening situation. Ava, it was like nothing I've ever seen before..."

"*Skyler.* The woman. The child. Where are they?"

"You... You passed out before you could save the mum with your adapts too. The child is fine. But the mum ... she's gone, Ava."

TWELVE

Ryder escorts us back through Haven, down the alleyways and roads, through the grey cells and buildings, through the whippings and beatings and the starving Marked. I try and let my mind wander to a place of peace, blocking out the world around me, and the task I'd just failed. I used to do this when I was so frightened that I couldn't cope with what was happening around me. Back when Mum didn't return that day, like she'd promised. Back when the world seemed large and strange.

Now, I find myself needing to do it again.

I am lying on the sand, feeling the rough pebbles and grains of the beach underneath me. I watch two children run and play. One of them is my brother and the other is the little girl in the pink dress, the one I saw on the day everything changed. I am happy. I am safe. Mutes don't exist. Skyler is there laughing and Mum and Dad and Kai and...

Suddenly I am surrounded by reality again. Too much reality.

Ryder pulls me into another road with a jerk when he realizes what I have seen – but it's too late. Something snaps. I lose control – of my own fear, of my feet under me. I collapse to the ground.

What I had seen was a man. He'd been so beaten he looked half dead. Just lying there on the ground. Guardians flanked him with guns so no one could aid him. He's just left there to suffer alone. An example of what happens when you don't follow the rules.

I slump into Ryder, and Skyler is crying too, but she is telling me to stay there, to keep fighting, to keep living, to not leave her.

But if this is my fate, why should I go on living – why should any of us? I shut my eyes. I shut out everything: the Guardians, Skyler, Ryder.

"Ava, we need to go. You need to get up." It's Ryder's voice, though I try to block it out.

The woman's face invades my mind again. Her screams for me to save her child. She was so selfless, and so brave in her last moments and I couldn't save her. I had failed.

"Please. You need to get up." His voice shakes.

"Ava, *please*." Skyler tries to pull me up. "If they see us here, like this, if you show them they can break you, they'll make you look at stuff like that all day. Just to tame you. Just to get you to do whatever they want you to do. Ava, Goddammit. *Get up."*

My gaze lifts to them both.

Ryder's eyes, looking into my own now they almost look ... amber. *Amber eyes.* My mind whirls. The Mute attack. He was the one. *He* was the Guardian who brought me to Haven. He was the one who brought me here to die.

No no no no no no no...

"GET OFF ME!" I scream. "GET OFF ME, YOU MONSTER!"

I tear myself from his grasp and run as fast as I can, all the way to the edge of Haven.

To the edge of my sanity.

THIRTEEN

Rain hammering down, soaking my clothes, pulls me into the present moment. Has it been hours or seconds since I tore myself from that monster's grip and had ran as fast as I could? No one had stopped me, or even given me a second glance. It was as if the grief on my face was too hard to look at. So they'd simply ignored it.

That man, beaten on the floor, the woman's face, pleading for me to save her daughter. I can't erase them from my vision. I rub my eyes until I see stars, until they start to leak, salty water engulfing my nose, my mouth, my lungs. I try to take a few more ravaged breaths but my lungs are no longer working in the way I want them to. I pivot into a deserted alleyway. It smells like urine and long-forgotten garbage that has been tossed away.

I wade through the stink and the discarded, forgotten, rotten items that no one wants anymore and I sit there. I curl myself up into the smallest ball I can. Maybe I can disappear. Maybe I can drown myself in forgotten things and maybe one day I, too, will become a forgotten thing.

"Ava! AVA!" I hear Skyler shout my name and run past, Ryder in tow. I do nothing to alert them of my presence. I sink further into the rubbish pile.

Minutes turn into hours. Still I sit, the rain soaking me, making me shiver to my core.

That woman. *Her child.* Her child who now does not have a mother. Thanks to me. I'd failed. I'd failed everyone.

"Ava?" I hear a soft voice.

I do not look up.

"*Ava.*" It persists. I hear rustles in the trash and see a figure take a seat next to me.

"Skyler and I have been looking everywhere for you," Kai says. I continue to stare straight ahead. "I heard what happened. I'm sorry. I'm so, so sorry."

"Kai." I say. My voice is shaky but I feel resolve in what I need to do. These few hours in the forgotten rubbish have finally given me clarity. On how to become forgotten myself. On how to make sure no one will get hurt by hand ever again.

"Kai. I need you to do something for me."

"Anything." He shuffles a little closer.

"I need you to kill me," I say calmly.

"Wh—what? Ava, I—"

"I need you to kill me. Or more people will die. It's because of me that a woman is dead and if I'm not here anymore he can't – he can't send me on any more trials. I can't hurt any more people. What I can do, Kai, it's *unnatural.* And I can feel my body – it has so much power. And I don't want it. This is the only way I can stop him."

"Ava." Kai gently pulls my face towards his own, his dark eyes alight with passion and understanding. "I know where we are – this place, it seems like there's no hope. Like there's no way we will get out. But Ava, you have to *keep going.* Don't you know that's the bravest thing you could possibly do? Keep living, Ava. Keep *fighting.*"

Tears roll down my cheeks. "Kai, I don't want to anymore – I can't. I'm broken."

"So am I." He searches my eyes and takes a deep breath as his own eyes grow clouded with pain. "I haven't told you much about before – before I got stuck here. My mum, she was the best person. She was so kind, the best mum you could ever ask for. My dad – he was not a good man. He – he used to beat me. And my mum. A lot. And, one day..." He swallows but continues on, "One day he beat her up so bad. And he made me watch. I was only twelve but I can still hear her screams, so clearly in my mind, as if it only happened yesterday. And he kept hitting her and hitting her and I begged him to stop and he wouldn't and—"

Now it was his turn to weep and tears pour down his own face, his brow furrowed, shoulders hunched. He continues on with the story, his voice a strangled thing. "I just wanted him to stop, he was *killing her.* So, I hit him on the head with the first thing that I could find – a rock. And he didn't wake up again. And it's all my fault. Ava – that wasn't your fault in there. And if I can keep going, with that kind of blood on my hands – so can you."

I had stopped moving, stopped breathing. This kind, gentle, boy who was not a fighter, but a healer, had fought for his mum's life. Even when it killed him inside to do it. His levity, his positivity; he'd had to fight for it. Every damn day. He'd fought to stay himself. To stay human. And he'd been through worse than us all. "Kai—" I went to speak, to apologize for all I'd done, for all that had happened for him, but he continues on.

"So, I won't kill you Ava. I *can't.* You're – you're all I've got now my mum has gone too. But ... I – I can sing to you. It's a song from *tangata whenua,* the people of this land. My mum used to sing it to me when

I didn't want to go on anymore. When I couldn't hold the weight of what I'd done – the music held it with me; it made me believe that it was going to be alright, in the end. Made me hope. It's *Pūngāwerewere*, a Māori song about a spider, weaving through life. We may be stuck in this web now. But one day, one day we'll get out of here."

"I asked you if you were a fighter, Kai, the day I first met you. You said no. But you're wrong. You fight with this." I place my hand on his heart.

He gently smiles and then slowly, quietly, he begins to sing. His voice is soft, and as the melody swells, so does his voice. He embraces me as he sings, and we stay there in the beauty and pain of his song. And slowly, ever so slowly, I begin to hope.

FOURTEEN

Today we are on City Protection.

To make sure no Mutes will ever get in, they say.

Bullshit. I say.

It's to make sure we never get out.

We are digging today; improving the moat that sits just before the electric fence that holds us all in here. They've reinforced it with traps. I shudder to think of the pain these atrocious metals and nails would cause another human. Some Marked have made a run for the fence, in an attempt at freedom, all had failed. If you didn't get hit by a trap, the moat was too deep to ever get out.

And then the Chosen could punish you themselves. Or, if they did not wish to kill you, they'd leave you there. That's only happened once in the time I've been here. I can still hear his moans of hunger and pain, until one day there were none. I wish they'd just killed him. A quick death would have been kinder. Less hard on his family.

If Guardians were seen by the cameras to be helping the Marked, they and their entire families in the luxurious Chosen quarters would be executed. I'd noticed that not all Guardians were the bloodthirsty monsters I'd originally thought them to be. Some were just ... surviving, I guess. Just yesterday, I saw one Guardian turn his head away when an older man gave his food to a young girl. Refusing food or giving it to your family is usually a punishable offence. They only give you just enough to survive because *they* want to decide when you die. They want to take that power away from you. If you decided to give your portion of food to a family member to keep them alive, it could be the death of both of you.

I watched in horror as the whole scene played out before my eyes, sure of the punishment the Guardian would give after seeing the old Marked man give a young girl his portion of food. I winced in anticipation of the beating, but it never came. The Guardian, a stout man with shoulder-length red hair, had walked around the corner just as it happened, but pretended he didn't see it. The older man inclined his head in thanks to the Guardian as he walked past, as if there were years of unspoken understanding, even *respect* between the men. The Guardian's eyes had not shown a flicker of recognition at what he'd just seen.

The length of a Guardian's hair can reveal how long they had been working in Haven for. The Marked have no hair, so we are nothing. This Guardian had long hair, so I knew it wasn't a rookie mistake. It had been deliberate. His ice-blue eyes pierced into mine, challenging me, daring me to turn him in. He turned on his heel and left me on the street, balking at what I'd just witnessed.

I am pulled back to the present moment at the aching pain in my back from the hours of digging. Sweat sticks to my forehead and I hear ragged gasps. I am stunned to realize they are my own. I feel dizzy and weak. I stagger a little and Kai glances over, frowning at me. He knows what will happen if I stop. We hadn't talked about the moment we'd shared just a few days ago. Where I'd almost ... I hung my head in shame thinking back to what I'd asked of him.

I shudder to think of the next trial White Suit has set for me. He seems to know the only way to motivate me to do his bidding is to put innocent people in danger. And he knows there is someone more important to me than anyone else in here. Skyler. I know in my heart that Skyler is in grave danger here, that she is next in his little mind game. My heartbeat quickens a little and I turn to see where Skyler is working. I carefully track the movements of every Guardian near her.

They can't hurt her if you can figure out how to get out of here.

That was the thought that had been running through my head since the second trial. Some part of me knows that's what White Suit had in store – the grand finale – but I won't let him get that far. Since that day, my mind has been spinning with possibilities; how in the hell I'm going to get her out.

"Kind of ridiculous, isn't it?" Skyler huffs from behind me. "The Marked are being worked to death, labouring over things that will only keep us here longer."

"Hush Skyler," I gasp.

Kai begins to talk loudly, knowing all too well what he's doing: "I wonder what would happen if everyone got their adapts back, or if we all attacked at the same time." Seething looks are shot our way as the Marked continue to work around us. "That's right," he continues, his volume increasing yet again, "Every Marked is too damn scared to stand up against the Chosen. Well, guess what – either way we're all dying!"

Fifty pairs of eyes are locked on us.

I throw him my best death stare. "Kai. You're going to get yourself killed. Shut. Up."

His shoulders sag a bit and he shoots a quick look at my drawn face. The purple bruise on my eye makes it difficult to look at him. "You spat in White Suit's face at the beginning of all this. Don't you remember that? He's the enemy, Ava, not me."

"I just know when to not be an idiot," I retort.

I see the hurt on his face and immediately regret what I'd just said. He'd bought me back when I wanted it to be over. His song made me *feel* again, feel something other than fear. And here I am tearing down *his* only way to fight back – speaking out. We stare at one another for a tense moment.

A shrill sound rings out over the field. Guardians emerge from seemingly nowhere, guns in hand pointed at the group of Marked around me. The Marked drop to their knees immediately. Skyler and I look to each other in confusion for a split second before Kai pulls us both down.

"What's happening?" I ask Kai, our previous fight forgotten.

"Inspection by the Chosen," he mutters. His head hangs low, avoiding all eye contact. Skyler and I follow his lead.

Footsteps sound and I recognize a voice. Involuntarily, I shiver.

Apex.

"You're talking too much today. All of you. You seem to forget the cameras can see you when you stop working. That means we aren't working you hard enough. Lazy and stupid, as always." The words are clipped and emotionless.

I see him out of the corner of my eye tossing a baton between his palms. Ryder is behind him, his square jaw tight. His eyes dart around nervously scanning the crowd for something, or someone, until they meet my own. With just one small shake of his head I understand his meaning.

No.

I realize it's a warning.

Apex has come here for something, something Ryder knows I'm likely to react to.

"Heard you've been causing trouble. Up." He grabs Kai's neck and pulls him to his feet.

My airways constrict with such force it's as if Apex had grabbed me by the neck, not Kai.

He's after Kai today.

The entire group has stopped moving: fifty eyes on the floor, praying they are not next. I glance to my right. A woman is crying and trembling, but she's careful not to make a sound. I glance to my left and Skyler's horrified expression mirrors my own. She grabs my hand and doesn't let go.

"Lick my boots clean, 1201." Apex seems amused by this game. His boots are drenched in mud. Kai squares up to him, looking him straight in the eye. There is no fear or trepidation in them, only stony courage knowing that this may be his last act of defiance.

"No." His gaze does not waver. I see him swallow.

Apex laughs as if Kai has just told him the best joke in the world. "Sorry?" His baton is moving faster between his hands now.

Apex knew how Kai would react, and he wants to make a point of it. I wonder if White Suit has tasked him with this, has seen how close I have grown to Kai since saving him in my first trial. Apex looks towards me and bares his teeth in something that resembles a smile, signalling this show was indeed meant for my eyes. As if White Suit has told him exactly how to break me. Exactly how to ensure that next time, I would not fight back.

"Well, sing for me, then." His gaze roams back to Kai and he cocks his head animalistically. His tone is mocking when he adds, "I have heard you have a beautiful voice. Our Doctor tells me you sing sometimes, to *boost morale*." Apex turns to the Guardians and throws back his head in a booming laugh. All of the Guardians behind him follow suit. Ryder does not. His gaze is fixed on Kai, stony as ever. Ready to watch whatever horror was about to unfold.

"Sing, 1201," Apex commands.

I stand to go to Kai's aid, but the hand placed in my own pulls me back. "No," Skyler whispers to me. "The more you show Apex and White Suit you care, the worse it'll get for Kai."

Kai's voice trembles. As if he knows what's coming, "No. Not here. Not for you."

Kai's singing was beauty. It was hope. It had been the thing that kept him sane in the darkest moments of his life. As it had for me. Kai's singing voice was the last gift his mother had given him. The sound of love. He would not surrender it. I knew he would die for it. Not for the singing itself, but for the hope it brought him, and others.

Thwack.

The sound of the baton hitting Kai's jaw was enough to bring me to my knees again. No sound comes from Kai as Apex begins to beat him. The lack of sound is somehow more horrifying. I scramble towards him, the dirt beneath me sending me flailing. I feel arms restraining me. Guardians push me to my knees again, grabbing my cheeks and pushing my face so I had a clear view of Apex hitting Kai, again and again. I see Skyler next to me, also restrained.

Thwack.

Another Guardian joins Apex in the beating.

Apex pins Kai down and pushes his neck further into the mud. He slowly squeezes and releases, squeezes and releases. Kai's eyes flutter as his consciousness begins to fade.

"NO!" I scream, clawing at the Guardians restraining me.

I know what will happen if I don't act right now. Right at this second.

And suddenly, I know what I need to do.

And my body responds. As if no matter how much venom they had injected me with, it didn't matter, not while he was in danger.

My adapts kick in. Razor-sharp thorns erupt from my arms. The Guardians that had been holding me scream in pain and release their grip, their hands riddled with the holes my thorns have made.

I run. I run for the fence and I don't look back.

I hear sirens whir, men shouting, but they don't shoot at me. Somehow, I know deep down White Suit has forbidden the Guardians to kill me, under any circumstances.

I look back, only once to the chaos behind me. In my mind's eye I can see White Suit examining me, his head cocked to one side. It's like I'm a piece of treasure. Like I'm a piece of a puzzle that he can't let go of.

My legs are already giving out, but I push on faster and harder, until the venom takes over my body again, rendering it useless. I've got to make a show, to take their minds off of killing Kai and onto me.

A sharp thud sounds as body hits body and I am on the floor. Dank, sticky mud covers my hands as I claw at the earth and continue to evade whatever has just hit me. I need to get to the fence. Getting to that fence is the only thing that will keep them from killing Kai. The thorns in my arms have retracted. I crawl as fast as I can but hands grab my legs and pull me back toward someone.

"Are you crazy?!" Ryder yells at me. He pins my arms down, stopping me from crawling any further. I close my eyes, willing for my adapts to come back again, for thorns to erupt and injure him, but nothing happens. I glance up at him, frustrated that my efforts are so damn pathetic. My adapts have gone again. The panic in his face is apparent. "That fence is electric. It could kill you in the state you're in right now! No matter how strong your adapts are!"

I spit, "Do you honestly think I care?" His rage stills into something that looks like sorrow when he sees the truth in my eyes.

Apex arrives, his face twisted into something that almost looks like excitement. "A runner. You almost reached the boundary. No one's done that in years. Remind me of the rules, Guardian. Doesn't that mean she should be sent to permanent testing?" Something in the way he says *permanent testing* makes me think it's not a place I want to be anytime soon.

"No." Ryder commands, dragging me up. "I have orders from the Doctor that she is not to be sent there or punished without his permission. I believe you do too, Guardian Apex." He lifts his chin, and suddenly he looks taller, broader.

Apex assesses him carefully. He looks like a child that's been denied his favourite toy. "It must have slipped my memory," he grunts. "Get her out of my sight."

FIFTEEN

"Where is Kai?" I ask for the seemingly hundredth time. "I need to see Kai." I try to squirm away from him. Ryder's grip is vice-like on my arm, pulling me relentlessly in the opposite direction of where we had just come from.

We dart through the streets, turning each corner so sharply that I feel dizzy. I dig my heels into the ground, my bare feet sliding across the gravel. Ryder feels my resistance and looks at the blood on my heels. Finally, he stops running.

"Where. Is. Kai."

"When are you ever not trying to be a martyr? Kai is fine. We need to get some distance between Apex before he changes his mind and comes looking for you." He growls: "I'm trying to help you."

He pulls me into a communal cell. It's not the one where Skyler and I are usually held. The women in there stare at us apprehensively. "Get out," he commands. They don't need to be told twice.

"Do you have any idea how stupid that was?"

"Yes. I did it for Kai. That's what people *do*. They protect each other. Not like any of *you* would understand that."

"You could have been sent to permanent testing or executed on site."

"I'm aware of that," I say through gritted teeth. "Now, let go of me."

"You need to tell me something and you need to tell me the truth. It is *imperative* you tell me the truth. Do you understand?" There's something about the panic in his eyes that makes me nod tentatively.

"Did you manage to avoid your injection this morning?"

I shake my head. There's no way to avoid it. They line us up every morning, first thing. There are checklists. No matter how hard I'd tried, it was next to impossible.

"So your adapts kicked in like that *without* an antidote injection like the Doctor gives you in your trials, *and* with the weakening serum still in your blood?"

I nod.

"Holy shit." Ryder runs a hand through his hair, shaking his head in disbelief.

"Why am I not dead?" I say. "What does White Suit want with me? Why does he want my family? Why is he making me do these trials?"

"He wants your family because it means a greater hold over you. You'd do anything for him with them here, right? You would tell him everything he needs to know about the Resistance. You'd take any trial he wanted you to." He glances toward the window, at the shouts coming from outside.

"But I don't know anything about a Resistance." I say.

"But he *thinks* you do, and that's all that matters. I have to go. They'll be looking for you soon. Ava, why didn't you think about what you were doing back there? The serum – or venom – whatever you call it; it wasn't enough to contain your adapts once your emotions truly kicked in. The Doctor – if he knows your stronger emotions cause your special adapts to kick in, even with the weakening serum in your body, he'll know exactly how to control you. He'll double your weakening dosage, and he'll want your family more than ever. He'll double the search party out there looking for them. Hell, he'll triple it."

My stomach sinks. That last ember of strength that had been inside me this whole time – I could have used it to break Skyler out of here. Why had it kicked in then? Why had no other horror I'd seen caused my adapts to push past the venom in my bloodstream?

My mind spins in confusion and frustration. My one chance at breaking Skyler out before the third trial *has been within me the whole damn time.*

Ryder's voice is gravelly and he speaks as quickly as he can. My mind struggles with concentrating on what he's saying but I force myself to focus on him. This could be the most valuable information I get in here.

"They'll be looking for you. I'll tell them I lost you in the streets. Go and find Kai, check he's ok. If anyone asks you, *do not* tell them you had your injection today. Tell them you avoided it on purpose. You'll be punished. But better that, then if he knows the truth. If he knows your emotions pushed you past your weakened state, and you over-came the weakening serum by yourself, it's over. Consider your friends and family dead already. He'll want to push you to your limits. To see what you're truly capable of. He will use them to do that."

"Why is he doing this to me?"

He ignores the question. "If you want to keep your friends alive, trust what I'm telling you. Or don't. It's up to you."

He is almost at the door before I say, "Why are you helping me?"

Ryder turns and looks at me for just a moment before he murmurs, "Go and see your friends, Ava."

And with that, he is gone.

SIXTEEN

I wake to the sound of screaming echoing through Haven.

It's not an unusual thing to be hearing, but this time it's different. My blood runs cold and my heart drops into my stomach. I know whose scream it is. I'd recognize it as if it were my own.

Skyler.

Guardians usually escort us everywhere, but as I leave my cell I shove past the Guardian standing there.

I hear a cry of indignation and then a grunt of anger. Footsteps are behind me.

I run as fast as I know how to.

I *need* to get to Skyler.

I dart in and out of the streets. Most Guardians that see me look at the man running behind me and shrug like it's his problem. Where am I going to go anyway? There's no way out of here. All the Guardian in pursuit will do is punish me for my disobedience. He is slowing, and I can feel my lungs burning, but I push on. The footsteps quieten, I turn to see no one behind me. I've lost him, for now.

The main square is where we saw that man who had been beaten so I head there first. I round the corner and screech to a halt. The square is filled with Marked. Guardians are stationed around the perimeter, guns in hand. The Marked are locked into place, immovable from fear. Fear that they might be next. I follow the direction of their gaze and my stomach plummets.

Apex grabs Skyler by her leg and drags her across the concrete, etching gravel into her cheek, towards White Suit's feet, which are planted on a podium above the crowd. Skyler screams as the gravel cuts through her face. She claws at the ground in an attempt to get away from him, but one of her hands won't move properly. Her shoulder looks uneven. I think he's dislocated it. I am frozen in horror for a few seconds. My body jerks into action.

I push forward, shoving bodies out of my path. Seething anger and hatred fill me. Life doesn't make sense anymore – not until White Suit is dead.

I will kill him. For the woman I couldn't save. For the prisoners who drop dead from exhaustion. I've never taken a human life before – but I will do it. For Skyler. For Kai. I will kill him slowly and painfully. And everyone standing in my path.

I burst forward from the crowd and run at Apex's back. I've got no idea how I'm going to stop him – but I don't care. Before I can move more than a few metres towards them, I am yanked back by both my arms and pulled out of the main square into a dark alleyway. Rubbish lays strewn everywhere across the alley. It smells of faeces and fear. Limbs fly as I try to fend off my attacker but he overpowers me, throwing me against the wall.

A hand clamps over my mouth.

It's Ryder. He shoves his body against me, sandwiching me between two immovable objects: him and the wall behind me. I try to scream, kick, stab and fight with everything I have to get him off me.

"Ava," he pants, frowning and grunting, as I kick him once again. It's hard for him to keep me still. I've thrown a good few kicks and punches and I've felt them hit home.

Good.

"You need to calm down," he says in a low voice. "Think rationally. Skyler's not going to be executed. She broke a rule and the Doctor is punishing her for it."

"I'll punish you, you ass—"

"Shut up and listen." His jaw tightens. "She will be beaten. That's it. This is a punishment not an execution. Don't get yourself killed for that."

"That's it?! She's *mine*," I growl. "They can't do that to her. Not if I have anything to say about it." But now I know Skyler is not going to be killed, my adrenaline begins to diminish. Maybe it isn't the best idea to try and kill the head Guardian in front of everyone with my bare hands.

"If you oppose a rule-break in here, it's immediate execution or permanent testing. Don't do it. We're going to need people like you."

"What does that even mean? Of course the goddamn Guardians need people like me, people who break the rules, so they can punish and kill some more."

His face is still, millimetres away from mine, and in this light he looks otherworldly. Almost, beautiful.

I shove that thought out of my mind. *Hard.* He is as cruel as the rest of them. I need to remember that.

"Ava." Ryder pushes me against the wall harder. "You have no idea what's coming. I need you alive. So try to find a way to stop getting yourself into trouble. For now."

"Get your hands off her," another voice growls. I turn my head slightly to see Kai has emerged from the crowd and entered the alleyway where Ryder and I are standing. Ryder releases me, and I collapse, sliding down the wall behind me. Kai meets Ryder's glare with a ferocity I'd never seen from him before. "Back away," Kai says slowly. "Now." His brow is furrowed. Kai is not Kai anymore. I have no idea why a boy who can't fight properly looks so intimidating, but he's doing damn well.

And then I see sense. *Skyler.* I need to get to Skyler.

I claw my way up the wall, finding strength in my legs to move. I place my body between Kai and Ryder, unafraid of the consequences. If Ryder wants me alive, that's good. I can use that new knowledge to my advantage and keep Kai safe. I push Kai back with my hands whilst never leaving Ryder's blistering gaze.

Never let an opponent out of your sight; be aware at all times. That had been my first fighting lesson with Mum.

I slowly back away, my still hands gripping onto Kai, willing him to follow my lead. Ryder's face gives nothing away. "Go," he says, his voice flat. "Apex is finished. Get your friend to the medical wing."

I need no further prompting.

I slip into the shadows after Kai.

SEVENTEEN

We find her on the street, lying in a dark pool of blood. I start shaking again when I turn her over and see what they had done to her face. They don't even give Skyler a nurse in the medical wing.

Nancy, the quivering little thing that gives us our daily injections, insists that it's against protocol to help rule-breakers: it's not her fault Skyler was disobedient, so off she scuttles down the dark hall.

I wonder what Skyler had done that had made White Suit so angry. I put the question to the back of my mind, and we place her on the bed. We are left to our own devices, given nothing to tend to Skyler's wounds but water and cloth to clean the cuts. She cries while Kai cleans her wounds. Her pain is my own. I squeeze her hand. "Keep fighting, Skyler. Like you told me, remember?" All I get is a groan in reply. She begins drifting in and out of consciousness, so I watch Kai as he works.

He is an excellent healer, his deft hands plastering over her cuts and bruises with balms and ointments he's helped himself to from the nurse's cabinet. His eyes glow with compassion and concern. His infectious smile is replaced with a more sombre expression. I wish I knew more about healing a thing and less about killing it.

I know a million different ways to catch game and kill birds with my bare hands, but Kai – he's different. He's gentle. I study his face for a moment, and then go back to making a note of every part of Skyler's. There is no scratch, no bruise, that I want to forget: it must all be committed to memory. I thought I'd never see her again when I'd heard that scream.

"You know, I'm glad that Guardian – did you say he was called Ryder? I'm glad he did it," Kai says quietly.

"Did what?" I ask, stroking Skyler's head.

"Told you not to help her. If you interfere with a command, you'll either be killed or taken to permanent testing."

I glance at him in confusion so he goes on, his dark eyes haunted. "You become their little experiment. They try out different drugs on you, like the ones they use on us, to cut our strength off. They keep testing how much your body can take till you die."

I reel back in disgust. "How do you know that's what happens?"

"They display the bodies after they finish with them." He shivers. "Does the job. Keeps everyone in a constant state of fear. Keeps the Marked docile so they'll be afraid to fight the nurses giving them the weakening injections. If you refuse, they send you straight to permanent testing or execute you on the spot. Depends what mood they're in that day."

The silence in which I process this information feels like an eternity. Kai's face looks pale, his expression haunted.

"There was this girl, Leah. She was my friend – my best friend. We got captured in the wild together. After… what happened with my dad, our families had made a small group, just us. I think Mum hoped that we would ... well, I guess it doesn't matter anymore." He swallows audibly. "Leah was sent into permanent testing." He mumbles out the story, his eyes far away.

"I was getting beaten. I was dying. For typical Kai stuff. Exploring in places where I shouldn't be – places out of bounds for Marked. Labs where the scientists were trying ... things. It was right after my mum had died in here. I was so upset, I think I wanted them to catch me. But Leah got in the way of the Guardians. She stopped them killing me, and she got taken in to testing for it. I killed Leah. My friend. I killed her. I wish ... I wish they'd just taken me instead."

His hands are shaking, and I lay my hand gently over his. "It's not your fault. She died protecting you; it was her choice."

"That's the worst thing, though," he sniffs. "I haven't seen her body displayed in Haven. That means they are still testing her, they are still torturing her." His brow furrows. He looks up toward the ceiling, searching for a memory, a feeling.

"I can't even begin to—"

I feel a nudge at my side. Skyler is alert again, the pain subsiding. Her eyes are bright and awake, her chest rising and falling as fast as a hummingbird's. I am amazed but also perplexed to see her so well. And she looks really happy – a little too happy for someone who's just been beaten up.

"Ave—Ava. You... You need to listen... I—" She is hysterical. She can't even breathe properly. I stroke her head to calm her.

"Shhh. Shhh. It's ok. You're safe. I've got you."

"N—No – listen. I found something. Something important," she says, her eyes darting around the room, checking we are alone.

"What is it?"

"White Suit. I had to ... clean his office..." she chokes out, her breathing ragged. "They found me hiding in there; that's why they beat me. But they didn't see me take this." She opens her hand to reveal a tiny bottle. I can't quite grasp the meaning yet, but I know this is something important – something she's kept safe in her palm, through her entire ordeal. I peer closer: it's bright green.

"I found it, just before they found me. This..." She gestures to the vial of liquid. "...is why they've got us here. *This* is what they've been working on. The antidote they used on you for the trials – this is the exact colour. I think it's the same thing they've used on you."

"What?" Kai blinks in surprise.

"And it was right there in front of me. So, I took it. But even better, the Chosen. They have a secret." She pauses, out of breath, almost too excited to continue.

I almost yell in frustration from the anticipation. "What is it?" I ask.

"The Chosen. All of them. White Suit. The Chosen who try and stay hidden from us in Haven. They were scientists before the Cull wiped everyone out, but these guys, they never went *through* the Cull. Just like White Suit told us; they locked themselves away before they could get sick, before anyone else could pass on the virus to them. The virus that happened twenty years ago that either mutated or killed you. They were the only ones who knew the Cull was coming."

"What are you saying?" Kai says, his excitement growing, a seed of hope in his voice.

"I'm saying," says Skyler impatiently, eyes gleaming, "they aren't immune to the virus that mutated us to our super strength. They're normal, like the humans before the Cull, the slower, weaker ones that needed heaps of food and water. They are exactly the same. They never adapted to survive, like we did. They're normal."

EIGHTEEN

Normal.

> *I can run twenty times faster than they ever could.*
> *I can lift them up with one hand.*
> *I can destroy them.*

Adrenaline begins to pump through my veins. And then I remember – the injections, what they've done to all of us. This must have been what all the injections were about. They can't control hundreds of people that are naturally five times their strength.

That is how they've controlled us: keeping us weak and afraid so we can't use our natural strength against them until they find a way to replicate our abilities for themselves. And then they can use the serum to make themselves stronger ... so *they* could survive out in the real world again, against the Mutes.

We have mutated to outlive the Cull – we have survived the worst cataclysm the world has ever seen. And they had wiped us of all of the protection nature had gifted us. They've broken us with the injections, and now we're weak – just like them. Whatever they had pumped through our body with those injections – it would be impossible to fight them like this.

My body is no more advanced than theirs right now. And the Guardians are twice the Marked in numbers, not to mention their guns and electricity and cameras. Who knows what other technology they'd held on to since the Cull?

"How did you find all this information?" I ask Skyler. "Isn't it … locked up somewhere? And what about Ryder? He's a Marked like us. But some of the other Guardians like Apex aren't. And how did you even sneak into White Suit's room long enough to learn about this stuff?"

"I'm small and I'm fast," she replies. "You know, I've always been able to just sort of … blend in. Even now, with the weakening venom, they barely noticed me. The Marked have to clean the rooms and offices, and if they're talking about anything important they just kick you out. But I stayed behind. I hid. There are no security cameras in their rooms. They aren't worried about their own. The Chosen had an entire meeting with me listening in." She giggles, despite the fact she'd almost been killed for it. "Who knows what would have happened to me if they'd found me then. They found me way after the meeting finished. Yeah; Ryder. That got me confused too. But I heard them talking in the meeting." She lowers her voice again as a few other Marked trudge past.

"The Chosen gave refuge to other humans in their circles who knew about the virus but didn't fancy their chances of beating it in the Cull. In that time, they were the wealthy, well-connected, the leaders of the world. They asked to seek refuge with White Suit and his committee of scientists, twenty years ago. They were promised safety for their families from the Cull in return for servitude to the Chosen's cause, for life. So, the Guardians brought their families here. Everyone that works under the twelve Chosen leaders – the cooks, the cleaners, the nurses, the kids. There are Chosen kids here – they are all just normals too. They don't have the mutated genes we do either, so for years they have been passing down their dud genes. Their weak genes."

"How is that even possible?" Kai's eyes are glowing with excitement. This is what we'd been waiting for. The final piece of the puzzle.

Skyler's wounds are weeping into her eye, but she wipes away the blood and continues on, frowning from the pain. "They promised to help White Suit in return for their lives and hoped that one day they might find a cure for their weakness." She gulps. "Well, the Marked that have joined the Chosen, they had to prove their worth ... by killing one of their own."

I gape at her. Ryder has killed another Marked. I shake off the sickening feeling; I have to stay focused.

"Ava, there's one more thing. On White Suit's desk ... there was a huge file. It was *massive*. That was the point when I got found. It had your name on it. And when I opened it, there was a photograph. The picture looked *exactly* like you, your age and everything. But it wasn't you. It ... it had the name Zara on it."

I forget how to breathe.

Zara was my mother's name.

My *mum* had been here?

My mind whirls in confusion. Mum and Dad had never told me of this place. Ever. If they had warned me, I might have known. I might have fought while I still had my adapts and managed to find a way out of here. White Suit said he'd never seen anyone like me before. But Mum had always been different too. She didn't have the special adapts that I do, but she'd always been stronger, and faster than anyone else we'd met out in the wild.

My brain feels scattered. I try to pull the pieces together. "Mum?"

Skyler nods solemnly. A thought hits me. "Wait. You were in White Suit's room? And this is his?" I point towards the vial of green liquid she is holding.

Kai interrupts. "You stole this from the Doctor's office? Don't you think he's going to notice that the thing he's been working on for who knows how many years is missing?" My stomach begins to twist in fear as I realize how right Kai is.

"Skyler, what have you done?" I say.

She sits up, attempting to back-track. "N-n-no. He won't notice. There were at least twenty vials of it. He won't notice one has gone ... will he?"

Kai explodes. "Of course he will! If they were in his room these vials must be different to the injections we get every day. They've got to be different or he wouldn't keep them so safe. You've just put every single Marked life in danger. Not just ours." Skyler's eyes well with tears as the realization overcomes her. Her fearlessness might have just killed us both. Might have just killed us all.

I look at them, dismay overwhelming me. Who knows how many other prisoners White Suit would torture in Haven to locate that vial? I would have to give myself in and tell them I took it. There was no other option.

Except maybe one.

1641

A Chosen nurse scuttles in. Her delicate hands are holding a small box that contains our daily injections. She is a small, stout woman with an upturned nose, and an air of superiority that all the Chosen seemed to exude.

"Identify yourselves," she commands. As taught, we all stand to attention. Skyler does too, slowly and with more effort than Kai and I. We rattle off the numbers on our necks that mark us as their property. "Your daily injection is due. I'll start with you, 1641."

She hides her fear of us well, but now I know their secret I can see it as clear as day. This must be why the Chosen hate us so much – at full strength, we could crush them in an instant. She taps the angry-looking needle a few times in silence, and I make a decision.

A decision not to let myself be controlled.

A decision to live or die trying.

I rally all my strength and launch a huge kick at the nurse's arm, knocking the needle high into the air. Her face contorts in horror, and she opens her mouth to scream, but not before I punch her, knocking her out cold on the ground. There is a dull thump as her head hits the concrete floor.

I catch the needle in my hand.

Kai and Skyler stand stupefied. Kai breathes out a low whistle, eyeing me appreciatively. "You. Are. Amazing," he breathes.

But there's no time for talking.

We need to run.

NINETEEN

"It needs to be you," Skyler says.

"No, Skyler. Don't argue, just take it – either of you." My hand shakes as I swap the vials of serum: the one that was meant to weaken us and the one that Skyler has obtained. I hold the needle out to them.

"Skyler is right, Ava. I have never seen adapts like yours before. Some people have particular gifts from the mutations since the Cull but your adapts, how they change to your environment. If this right here is what we think it is," he takes the syringe from me and examines it, "then it needs to be you. You're the strongest of all of us. And if anyone is going to get all three of us out of here alive, it's you."

"No. I want you – either of you – to take it. It'll keep you strong and get you out of here alive."

Skyler and Kai throw a glance at each other and I see a shared thought flash through their eyes. But before I can catch up, Skyler shrugs and says, "Sorry Ava." She sweeps her leg out, knocking me to the ground. In a second, she has me pinned.

Kai looks apologetic as he stabs the needle into my arm and pushes the green liquid out of sight and into my body. "You'd see our point of view if you weren't so damn stubborn." He grits his teeth. His face is hard, unwavering. I start a little as I feel the cold venom enter my bloodstream.

But instead of the all-too familiar feeling of drained energy, and weakened senses, a surge of energy radiates through my body. It's a familiar feeling. I'd missed this energy, but I haven't known just how much until now.

My eyesight is immediately sharper – finally clear again. My hearing perks up. I hear both screams of pain and gruff orders from the Guardians – hundreds of voices gurgling up from Haven. The voices are everywhere. They engulf my senses. I am shocked at the overwhelmingly sharp reality – how different Haven is now; how blurry it's been for so long.

"Thanks a bunch," I mutter, sarcasm dripping in my voice, furious that neither of them has their own adapts back. But a glimmer of clarity forces itself upon me; their logic did make sense. And now it's up to me to keep them safe.

I look up to see the surveillance camera that has been staring at us from the corner. I rip it down from the wall and crush it with one hand.

We've only got a few short minutes before somebody notices it's no longer working. I have no time to consider the consequences of what I've just done. We grab everything in the medical wing that could be of use to us and stuff it into a small bag Skyler has located.

"Right – so what about everyone else? Who else shall we try and break out? The kids? What can we do?" Kai asks and my heart sinks.

My main concern had been getting these two out alive. Of course he thinks of others before himself. A wave of shame washes over me. The way I'd grown up – survival had been everything. He'd been brought up differently.

"Kai..." Skyler's face drops and she shakes her head.

"We've got to help them though. We can't just leave them here," he responds.

"And we won't." I interject. "Kai, I have to get you two out. It's too risky to try and take women, children, anyone not as fit as you two. A big group will be easily tracked and slow moving. The only way I see this working is with just us. I'm sorry." My words are tactical and not up for debate and Kai knows it.

"The Resistance," Skyler says, her eyes lighting up. "What White Suit has been going on about. There has to be another group out there. A group that are trying to help the Marked and set them free. I've heard whispers of it from all of the Marked. If we make it out of here alive, we could find them – we could tell them what we know."

Kai's brown eyes look to me. A longing. A pleading. I concede: "Kai, I swear to you on my little brother's life. If we make it out of here alive, we'll go to the Resistance. We will tell them what we know. We will help break these people out of here. But right now, we need to *go.*"

An ear-splitting sound radiates from above us and a monotonous voice rings through the room over the loudspeaker: "All Marked report to the main square for questioning."

They must have discovered the vial is missing. "We need to move. Fast," I say. I grab the backpack Kai is holding and swing it over my shoulder.

"If we're leaving, we need to take Leah with us too." Kai looks desperate.

"What?" I say through gritted teeth. I focus on my breathing, trying to calm my temper. If he keeps trying to save people, and slowing us down, we'll be dead within minutes.

"Leah. The girl I was telling you about. She's still locked up in permanent testing. I know she's there. I have to find her. She'll die if we don't take her with us."

I weigh my options. We currently have the element of surprise. We can maybe get out of here, but only if we move now. I shake my head. "I don't know how long this serum will last in my body. I don't know how long I'll stay strong enough to take on the Guardians. It's too dangerous."

Kai's face crumples and it kills me a little. "Ava, please. We have to try. I owe her my life."

I sigh. Boys and their feelings. "Fine," I concede sharply. "Skyler, you need to take us to White Suit's rooms, where you found these vials of serum. If we're going to have any chance at getting to Leah, we'll need to get you guys back to full strength too, and we'll need to get one for her. If she's weak, she'll be a liability." I shoot a look at Kai to prove a point and he nods his head so furiously that it looks like it'll fall off.

"She won't be." he confirms.

I sneak a look outside the room, down both corridors, and confirm to the others it is safe to move. It's still dark outside. The hallway of the medical wing is still. Most of the Guardians must have escorted Marked to questioning in the courtyard. Well, I'm guessing that's where everyone is. Hopefully, they are more focused on the stolen items than on *our* immediate whereabouts.

We jog through the corridors as quickly and silently as possible, making our way through the maze of buildings. I feel my legs return to their normal pace, but Skyler and Kai can't keep up with me. Their faces are red and their bodies heaving with exertion. It's barely a jog for me. I don't feel the least bit tired or out of breath. "Keep up," I order.

Left, right turn, left again.

Behind me the ragged breathing increases; they're already wearing out, their energy diminished because of their injections. We need more options. As we round the corner, I see a Guardian. I step quickly aside, but he's already on alert.

Sensing danger, the burly Guardian swings his fist towards my jaw, but I am too fast – his movements seem to happen in slow motion. All too easily I duck out of the way, my fist slamming into his gut with such immense force he shoots backward a few metres, landing on his backside, retching in pain. I'm in front of him in less than a second. I snatch the rifle out of his stupefied grasp and strike him over the top of the head with it. He falls to the floor with a thump, unconscious. Blood spurts from his head wound. It paints the grey concrete in a small pool around him. I drop the rifle and motion to Kai to aid me and grab one of his arms, dragging him into the shadows.

I feel like vomiting or crying. Possibly both.

I have no idea how we are going to save Leah, let alone escape ourselves. Now we're taking Guardians down, there will be no going back from this. I start to regret this crazy idea ever forming in my head as I scan Skyler's and Kai's worried faces.

"Stop," a voice orders. When I turn, my breath catches in my throat. Ryder is standing directly in front of us, blocking me from our only exit. The barrel of Ryder's rifle stares directly at me, menacing, still and sure.

There's no explaining our way out of this. Kai and I still have the Guardian lying limply in our hands. I survey the options around me: I can't get to rifle I'd discarded to lift the Guardian without Ryder seeing and shooting first. My chest feels tight at the thought of shooting him, but I shake off the thought.

Skyler is frozen next to us, crouched over our bag. There's a scalpel in it but there's no way she can get to it, so she's unarmed too. Her hands hover above her head in a sign of mercy, her eyes wide in panic.

"You're trying to get out of here, aren't you?" He rolls his eyes. "I thought I told you to keep a low profile." Ryder slings his rifle onto the strap behind his back, letting it rest there. He sounds like he's chiding a child.

I splutter, "Aren't you gonna ... shoot?"

"Well," he shrugs nonchalantly. "*My* plans are now screwed, thanks to you three. I guess I'm going to have to help you instead."

"W—what?"

"I'll explain later, but right now we need to go. Grab the gun." He nods towards the discarded rifle and hands a knife to Kai, and another of his handguns to Skyler.

I snatch the rifle off the floor and weigh the weapon in my hands. As I slowly lift it towards Ryder's face his eyes cloud in shock. He matches my gesture with a weapon of his own trained on me. Our movements happen in less than a second, and we stand locked in position, each threatening the other with deadly force.

"How do we know you aren't with them?" I ask.

"You don't," he counters. "If you want your friends out of here and safe, we need to leave. Now. And the only way you're going to get out of here alive is with my help."

I remain frozen, my weapon trained on Ryder.

"Look," he says. He places his weapon on the ground and fishes out some keys from his back pocket. "These are the keys to a Guardian truck. I also have a key card that will get us out of the front gate. The only way out is one of these, if you touch the fence, you're dead." He slides them across the gap between us on the ground, standing slowly, careful not to startle me.

I never drop the gun or my eyes from his face. "Skyler, get the keys," I order.

"It's parked at bay 35."

A realization: "I can't drive." *Shit.*

"That's why you need me. Ava, think rationally just for a second. Why would I be doing this if I was with them? How would it further *him*?" We both know who he's talking about. "Think about it. Please." His hard features have softened as his head tilts to the side. I push aside my distrust and for a moment and see a young man standing before me, bare and vulnerable. He has no defence right now; isn't that enough for me to believe he is telling the truth?

Every fibre of my being is screaming at me to not believe him, but somehow I do.

"We need to find a girl. She's in the permanent-testing cellblock." I shoot a potent look to Kai whose eyes glow with gratitude. Or maybe he's just excited to see Leah. I try to shake the thought off but it crawls back under my skin, trapping itself inside my heart. I don't have time to examine it – not now – so I leave it there on its own. I turn back to the moment at hand.

"Ryder, you're with me," I say, "We'll find Leah. Kai, Skyler, you get the car and confirm our escape route. Ok?"

Kai objects: "You're trusting him? He's one of *them*, Ava."

"We have no choice."

"I can't go with you, Ava," Ryder says. "I have to get the truck with Skyler. They'll see he isn't a Guardian," he says, scanning Kai's obvious Marked clothing.

"I don't trust you with them. You're with me," I insist.

"Fine. Then we need to switch." Ryder pulls off a thick vest – it looks as if no bullets are getting through that sucker – and black shirt. Kai follows suit, removing his grey tattered shirt.

Both of their bodies are supple, capable. I realize I have to be watching to notice that sort of thing and shoot my gaze to the floor in response. They throw each other a vicious stare whilst trading the necessary clothes. Skyler gives me an amused look, one eyebrow arched.

"Identify yourself as a Guardian with Skyler as your prisoner. If anyone asks, say you are usually on Chosen bodyguard duty. Chosen bodyguards and Marked Guardians don't usually interact, so they won't expect to know who you are if that's the case. Go to the bay and meet us outside of Permanent Testing Block A in fifteen minutes, ok?" Ryder orders.

Fifteen minutes.

In fifteen minutes we could be captured or free from this hell.

I could see my family again.

Xander, I'm coming.

"Let's go," I say. I walk towards Ryder with my gun at the ready.

"Be careful," Skyler warns.

"Always," I reply as I slip into the darkness after Ryder.

TWENTY

We move in stunned silence. My breath catches as I hear the heartbeats of those walking past me. Do I look different with the antidote in my system? Do I move differently? I try to slow my steps and remember what it felt like to be drained of strength. Slowly, the number of Guardians walking past us subsides.

Ryder indicates towards a steel door, giving me a key that has appeared seemingly from nowhere.

"The permanent-testing room is through there," he says. "All Guardians were called to the square for questioning so there won't be anyone there. Hurry."

I spin on my heel and jog towards the door. I fiddle with the keys. I've never used these things before. I finally manage to get the door unlocked. It smells stale with a sharp tang of blood. The room is completely black. I pause as my eyes adjust and make my way through the building. Panic surges through me as an absurd series of thoughts spread through my brain like wildfire. What if this is a trick? What if Ryder's whole act is to lure me in here for White Suit? What if the Chosen are waiting in here for me? And then, through the darkness comes a small voice.

"Hello?"

"Are you Leah?" I ask.

"Yes. Who... How do you know I'm here?" she stammers, her soft voice echoing through the thick darkness.

"Kai's my friend – he sent me. We're getting you out of here. If you want to live, come with me right now."

I hear shots outside, slicing through the silence of the room. *Shit.* They know.

"Hurry!" I grab her by the shoulder roughly and pull her into the light through the doorway. I almost gasp when I see her. Even with the gashes on her face, Leah is beautiful: dark mahogany skin with small rounded features, perfectly aligned and proportioned.

Focus, Ava.

I take her hand and we make our way through the cell block, corridor after corridor until we get to Ryder at the front door of the cell block. He aims and sends another round of shots towards the Guardians firing at us outside. I slide into place next to him, taking my own rifle in my hands. It's heavier than I thought it would be. I pull the trigger and almost lose control, I didn't think it would move that much.

"Hold it closer to you. Use your shoulder to keep it steady," Ryder shouts, never taking his eyes off his targets.

I obey, but still don't manage to hit anything with it. Where are knives when you need them?

A large, dark truck pulls up, blocking the shooting for a few seconds. We sprint towards it and the door slides open in a rare moment of divine timing. The truck isn't being damaged by the guns.

"Bulletproof," Ryder explains. I smile in approval.

I fling Leah into the van, ducking bullets as they fly a few inches past my head. Kai hauls her towards him and they embrace quickly, before our situation forces them back to the reality at hand.

I am standing just outside the van, and I roll to avoid more shooting. I can see Guardians making their way closer towards Ryder, who is still slightly behind me. I shoot and then stare in horror as I see one of my bullets hit its target, landing square in the chest of the man closest to Ryder; the flesh of the man is ripped apart with the force of the shot.

Nausea grips me as I realize what I have done.

Ryder shoots the rest of them down, running backwards, sure to avoid a position of vulnerability.

All I can do is stand there.

And then he's in front of me, yelling something, loud and fierce. I can't breathe.

Ryder takes hold of my arm roughly, his grip squeezing my flesh so hard it brings me back into the present moment. I am dragged towards the door; Ryder is shooting all the way, not stopping till we reach the van again, together. The door is thrown open. I am flung inside first, and Ryder follows, slamming the door with a loud *thwack*. "Go!" he yells to Kai who is now at the wheel.

The dark buildings and empty streets blur as we race through them.

"Faster," Ryder says. "Haven will be in lockdown at any moment now." Through the adrenaline and fear, I notice that something is missing.

"Where's Skyler?" I ask Kai.

"Ryder, take the wheel," Kai commands.

"Oh piss off, you really think I'm gonna take orders from—"

"Take it." The authority in Kai's voice offers no room for objection. Ryder grabs the wheel and awkwardly swaps places with Kai, muttering under his breath. Kai climbs back to where I sit stupefied in the van next to Leah. We are both being thrown from side to side as Ryder attempts to dodge Guardians, who are pursuing close behind and shooting at our truck.

I block out the noise and the erratic movement and focus. "Kai," I say, steadying my voice. Dread drips through my body like ice. "Where is she?"

"She's gone."

"Gone? What the—the... What the hell do you mean, gone?" I stammer. "We need to go back and get her, we need to turn around—"

No no no no no ... this isn't happening this isn't real it can't be real.

I am turmoil. I am delirium. I am agony. I can't keep my limbs from convulsing and shaking. Tears begin to blur my vision. "Is she—" I start. "She's dead, isn't she?"

Kai pulls me close to him, forcing my arms against his chest. His dark eyes are the only thing I can hold on to, the only thing I can comprehend. They are full of sorrow. The world dims and sharpens simultaneously. Kai's eyes search mine. When he speaks I can barely hear him. "One minute she was with me, then she ... she thought it would be a good idea to slash the tyres of the other trucks so no one could follow us after we escaped and ... I heard shots. I heard ... a scream. And then silence. And she didn't come back." He swallows hard, his voice strained. "I'm sorry."

"We—we need to go back. To get her body. I need to say goodbye."

Ryder drives on, never taking his eyes off the road, swerving through the alleys and streets, all the while aiming his gun and shooting out the window. "I'm sorry Ava," he says in a voice I find remarkably calm. "But if you don't want a funeral for yourself, grab a gun and start shooting."

She's gone. Skyler is gone.

I try to repeat the words in my head, to make sense of it.

"I mean it," Ryder says. "We've got company."

TWENTY-ONE

I open the window feeling the cool breeze on my boiling-hot face and I do the only thing I know how to do.

Destroy.

I fire at several trucks behind us, splitting open tyres, sending them flying, shattering glass, blowing engines.

I am possessed. I am merciless.

I know I won't stop until someone physically pulls me from my task. The guilt I felt for killing that man before – it's gone. They've taken Skyler from me forever and they will pay a hundred times over.

"The gate! It's already closed!" Leah wails.

"If we drive into that, the truck is ruined and we're dead." Ryder says, not taking his eyes off the road ahead of him.

Before I can think about what I'm doing, I've launched myself out of the truck window I'm running alongside it. I keep pace with our truck, glancing behind me to others that Skyler didn't destroy in time before she ... I banish the thought from my mind. These people had taken her from me and they would pay, but first, we have to get out of here alive.

My muscles burn as I overtake our truck. I gain more and more ground, not quite believing the speed my body has achieved. And then I'm at the gate. As I touch it, I feel the electric shocks course through my body, shocks that would have once killed me – now they are nothing but annoyances as I peel back the metal gate as if it were a branch in a forest.

I feel a jolt and look down. There's a piece of metal there. I think it's called a bullet. My skin has adapted into silver scales around the area of the bullet. I peel the bullet out, the pain distracting me only for a moment before I continue with my task.

Push. Push through, Ava. I can hear Skyler's voice in my mind. I know she'd want me to get out, to be safe.

The gap I have made in the gate is just enough for our truck to hurtle through. I release the metal and it springs back, knocking into the trucks pursuing us. Ryder offers his hand and pulls me into the window I've just broken.

"How did you do that? How have your adapts become so advanced?" He looks concerned, as if piecing something together, something he can't quite work out.

"Um, guys. Maybe save the chit-chat for later?" Kai, who is now at the wheel, gestures at the sky and I see the most terrifying thing yet.

A mechanical monster. It's high in the air. I've never seen anything like it before. It is making deafening noises with sharp knives above it moving in a merciless circle, miraculously keeping afloat above us.

The mechanical monster stares down at us cruelly, as if it already knows our fate. It keeps firing at our truck, attempting to puncture something vital for our escape route. My ammunition has run out and

I release the gun from my hungry grasp, chucking it back to Ryder. I watch keenly as his deft hands add more bullets to the gun, locking in a new round.

"I'm sorry about Skyler," he repeats.

I avoid his face entirely, determined not to let him see through the hardened exterior I have restored. "How are we going to get rid of it? It's almost burst the tyres about five times now."

Leah is in the front with Ryder, weeping, curled into a small ball of unhelpfulness. Looks like this will be up to Kai, Ryder, and I. She's been through a lot today, but I can't help but feel spiteful towards her. It's because of our attempt at saving her that Skyler is... If it hadn't been for her, maybe Skyler would be...

Ryder passes the gun back to me, slowly and carefully, his eyes never leaving mine. I know he's looking for reassurance. I can't offer any, but I take the gun and nod. His jaw is tense as he moves towards the window and aims again at the Guardians above. I watch as his mouth drops and his eyes widen until they are almost out of their sockets. I turn to look out of the window too, my arm held stiff and ready to fire.

But I don't need to fire.

Because it's Skyler.

She's alive.

TWENTY-TWO

Apex has Skyler positioned by the door of the flying machine above us, precariously balanced in front of him, ready to drop her into oblivion. He recognizes me as reach my hand out to her. As our eyes meet, he mouths the unmistakable words that I somehow knew were coming.

"You." He points at me. "Exchanged. For her."

White Suit wants me back. And he'd sent the one thing that would achieve that.

Ryder sees the small exchange, and he realizes what is about to happen. He reaches for me, understanding my intentions, "NO!"

But it's too late. I've made my decision, and I'm sure as hell not going to let Skyler get killed again. I kick Ryder hard in the stomach to loosen his hold on me and I fling myself out of the open window, tumbling onto the gravel below. Over and over I roll, biting through the pain and protecting my head as much as I possibly can, until my body grinds to a halt. I can feel the antidote diminishing in my body.

That stunt with the gate must have dredged the last reserves of it. The pain I couldn't feel before – I can feel it more than ever.

My head pounds. I look down with dread at what has become of me. Not too bad, I'm surprised to see. A few bruises here and there. Not that it matters, I'm sure White Suit will kill me as soon I returned to Haven with Apex – what's a few scratches now?

Above me, the mechanical monster hovers loudly. No trucks have followed – they must still be stuck at the gate. Good. Apex throws a rope out and shimmies down it swiftly, along with Skyler tied to him, hanging in his arms helplessly, her hands and mouth bound. She recognizes me and her face begs me silently with all the words in the world. I should turn back to the truck, her eyes tell me; I should leave her here. I shake my head once, twice in denial.

No way in hell. I have already failed once at protecting her and I won't make that mistake again.

Apex smiles sickeningly at me.

I see on the horizon, from the corner of my eye, that our getaway truck has stopped, and is now circling back towards us. Kai is driving back towards the danger here – towards Apex and the hovering monster. I look up and see the controller of the machine staring down below him at me. His gun is trained on me too. I am completely stuck.

I look around for options. There's my gun, just off to my right. It hasn't landed too far away from me. I crawl as fast as I can to collect it. I grasp it firmly in my hand and fluidly spin around, aiming it straight at Apex's head.

But Apex is already one step ahead of me. He's suspected this move would be my next. He is holding onto Skyler firmly, positioning her directly in front of him as his own personal human shield. The way her body is protecting his own, there's no way I can kill him without injuring her, too. I'm not confident enough with this whole gun thing to guarantee her safety, and he knows I won't risk hurting her. *Dammit.* He grips her arm tightly and pulls it upward it around her back. She cries out in pain. From here, it looks like he's dislocated her shoulder again. My finger flexes on the trigger.

"Put it down," he commands firmly.

I obey.

"Now make your way over here."

I grimace. There's no way I'm going that easy.

I say in a voice as steady as I can make it, "And how do I know that you'll give her up if I agree?"

Skyler tries to talk but the material Apex has shoved in her mouth stops her from making words. I know she's telling me to run, so I shake my head.

"Ava!" Kai and Ryder have jumped out of the truck and are now sprinting towards me. Leah peers out from behind the truck's door.

"Stay back or the bargain is off and they both die!" He shoots a few bullets near them on the ground to prove his point. They both halt, barely a few metres away from me, their hands suspended in the air in a sign of submission.

My breath comes in ragged gasps as I begin to picture the reality of the rest of my life. How long will White Suit keep me alive? I swore to myself in Haven that I wouldn't crack, that I wouldn't let them break me. But I'd seriously begun to doubt my strength during my time there. Life with White Suit would be more than unbearable. It might just kill me.

But I look around at my friends, and at my options, and I realize I have to go with him. Even if I lose my mind in the process. This is what it takes to save Skyler.

My voice shakes, betraying my decision. "Ok, I'm … I'm coming towards you. Just don't hurt her. I will come back with you to Haven. Just … please don't hurt her."

A glint of reflection from Kai's boot catches my eye, and I realize I know what it is. Ryder had given him a knife, back in Haven. I watch as he moves slowly, putting his hands on his head, and making his way to the ground, as if to show his lack of threat.

Apex chuckles to himself whilst watching Kai. I seethe as I see how much he's enjoying the small victory of submission. "Even mutants like you can't dodge bullets," he spits.

"No, that's true," I agree as I step closer towards him. A small nod from Skyler indicates she's clocked my plan. "But neither can you. Kai, now!"

It all happens so fast. We move deftly, simultaneously.

Skyler spins and knees Apex hard in his groin and he doubles over in pain. Kai grabs the knife from his boot and throws it to me, hilt-first. Ryder lunges for my gun on the ground and takes the flying machine above us down with a single, loud crack. I think he's hit something important to its survival. The whole contraption explodes loudly with the heat radiating onto us, erupting in licks of flames as it begins its descent towards the ground.

As the machine falls to the floor, I do what I have been dreaming of doing since I arrived in Haven.

Aiming quickly and with precision, I throw the knife. The glint of silver flies through the air before hitting its target; Apex's chest. His sharp intake of breath seems to echo louder than the explosion above.

Apex falls with a thud, blood spraying as his skull hits the concrete. Then his body crumples and grows still. I suddenly have an odd premonition, as I watch Apex die, that this will be the only peace I will be getting for a long time, however strange and twisted this peace is.

Kai breaks the silence. "We did it!" He hoots in exhilaration. He runs to Skyler, lifting her high in the air. She laughs shakily, as if unsure of the right reaction.

"You know," Ryder says, strolling over to me. "If there was any chance that the Doctor wasn't going to search for us after we escaped, it's gone now."

"I know."

"You know this puts you and Skyler in even more danger?"

"I know." I gaze up into his face and grasp his hand in comfort, in gratitude. If it wasn't for him, we'd be dead. His eyes widen in surprise, his body rigid as if he's not quite used to human contact. Our breathing falls in time with each other's.

"I know," I breathe.

TWENTY-THREE

We stand at a distance, taking in the scene before us. The flames engulf our truck, and the flying machine Ryder has destroyed. The inferno illuminates the darkness, the moon above glaring down upon us.

"I still think it was a dumb idea," Kai says. "We could have used the truck. We'd get there faster."

"We don't want to take any chances," Ryder says, wiping an angry gash just above his eye nonchalantly. "I won't risk it. Guardians are great trackers. We're going to have to take the longer way, the harder way to track. On foot. It's a few days' walk to the Resistance base. It was called the Carter Observatory before the Cull. It's the safest place we've found in years."

"We've?" I splutter. "You're part of the Resistance?"

He shrugs in response, "Surprise," He grins. His face grows solemn again with the task at hand. "No trucks. I won't risk them being compromised for a quicker journey." Kai glares at him but says nothing in response.

Up until now, the idea of a resistance force has just been a vague reality that White Suit had tried to beat out of me – not something remotely real. This is news to me but somehow, it clicks everything into place, it makes sense.

Ryder continues, "And anyway, once we start getting our adapts back, we'll move a lot quicker. It shouldn't be too difficult."

"Will we really get our strength and speed back? All of our adapts?" Skyler glows at the prospect of our bodies becoming durable and athletic again.

"Yes. A couple of days more of feeling like this and the serum should be out of our systems – and we will be back to fighting fitness," Ryder replies. Then, as if to add extra reassurance, he says, "Back to normal."

Still watching the inferno off in the distance, a sudden wave of nausea grips me. Breath leaves my body and I almost collapse onto the concrete road. Next to me, Kai senses what is coming and grabs me, taking my weight before I can fall. His arms never leave my waist as he pulls me a little closer, running his fingers along my head, through my hair. There is warm blood trickling down my scalp, and only when Kai touches my head do I realize he's looking for the cause.

"You ok?" he says.

"I—just... um... Yep, yes I'm fine."

"No, you're not." He searches my face worriedly.

Leah touches my forehead, her cool hand feeling like bliss on my skin. "She's burning up," I hear her say.

Ryder doesn't even look. His eyes are scanning the horizon, his mind on something else. "She'll be fine," he says. "The antidote she took must have just taken a toll on her body. I don't know if they've ever risked taking such a high dosage themselves in fear of it killing them. There could be side-effects." He begins to lead the way, toward the tree line just ahead of us. "Get her up," Ryder adds abruptly. "We need to keep moving." I can tell he is itching to leave this place, in fear of what might already be in pursuit.

Kai stands next to me, still holding me up. The dizziness is overwhelming. "No," he says firmly. "She needs to rest."

I stagger as I push myself away from him, but I am determined to stand on my own two feet without aid. I push the nausea back down. "No, no I'm fine. Ryder's right, let's keep moving," I say.

Skyler squeezes my hand gently and I smile back, wrapping her in my arms for a moment. I still can't comprehend how lucky I am to have her warm body standing strong next to my own. My friend, my sister. She is here with me, safe and sound. I silently swear to myself that I'll never put her in a situation like that again. That I will be there for her.

At least I know now what has to happen next.

"You guys go ahead to the Resistance," I say. "Skyler and I need to leave. I do want to help you guys. All of you. But we need to go back to my family. We never came back for them, that day we were out hunting."

It seems like a lifetime ago, facing that Mute. But I've been counting the sunrises. Only fifteen have passed. Xander knows enough about setting snares to have survived this far. But I don't want to risk leaving it any longer. They'll be worried sick. And if Xander stumbles across a Mute...

I needed to get home as fast as I could.

They look horrified. I don't blame them. I probably seem unpredictable. Maybe even unreliable. But family comes first.

"But—" Kai interjects, but I don't let him finish.

"I need to make sure they're safe. I might not have told White Suit where they are, but he'll still be looking for them. He thinks they're with the Resistance, or he thinks they *are* the Resistance. I don't know what he wants with them but I need to go back to protect them, to let them know they are being hunted. They're too weak without me."

Ryder steps towards me, his amber eyes now dark with irritation. "I thought you were going to help me." He blinks twice. "Us. The Resistance."

I try to think through my slowed state. My stomach is churning; it feels like acid burning my insides.

"So, if you were part of the Resistance, why were you at Haven?

"My assignment was to infiltrate the Chosen by becoming a Guardian. . I'm a – how do you call it ... a double agent. Trust me," he says darkly. "It wasn't my idea."

My own exasperation bubbles to the surface without warning: "So, you just sat by, and let those other Marked, your own people, die?"

"It wasn't like that. I was following orders. A soldier follows orders from his superior no matter the personal cost. I made a promise to someone." His voice trails off as well as his gaze, and I see how his face looks gaunt, tortured by my words. "I made a promise to my dad. Well, he's as good as my dad, Thomas. He broke me out of Haven when I was young, trained me up. Led the Resistance to an almost victory and then..."

I finish connecting the dots: "White Suit killed him."

He swallows, "Yes."

Skyler pipes up, "So how did you become a Guardian if..."

"Look, that's not important right now. I had to do that, or White Suit would have found my people by now. I had to keep them safe. Like you're trying to keep your family safe."

Leah speaks slowly, quietly, her eyes darting around the tree line, as if expecting an attack: "We might have escaped the Chosen and the Guardians, but we aren't safe, and we never will be until they're dead. The Resistance is our shot at ending this, Ava. That's what Kai and I always talked about. If we ever escaped, we said, we owed it to the other

Marked in there to help them. To take Haven down. And now we have escaped. So..."

"I know. But..." I see the glassy eyes of my brother, my father's weakened state. "I can't just leave them. They already think I'm dead. I need to keep them—"

"You know, for a smart girl, you're sounding like a bit of an idiot," Ryder says.

"Excuse me?" I splutter.

"Did you not just hear anything I said?"

"Don't patronize me. I was—"

"We're already going to have to swim upriver to lose the other Guardians that are sure to be coming after us by now, so they can't track us. If you lead them back to your family then you're putting them in even more danger. They can track you easily if you don't know how to throw them off the scent, like I do."

I step closer to him, my fists balled at my sides. "I'm not the one who killed one of my own to pretend I was a Chosen."

Ryder looks furious. "You have no idea what happened or—"

Leah and Kai push in between us, almost dragging us apart. I am going to do whatever I want – what I need to do – and no unsaid promises to him are going to stop me.

"Calm do—" Sudden nausea overcomes me and this time I fall to the ground, hard. Stars are everywhere; my mind is foggy.

"Ava, are you—"

"I'm fine," I grunt as I stagger to my feet.

Skyler pulls me away from the others, her eyes begging me to see reason. "You're not well. Your body is in shock. Let's just get to the Carter Observatory, get you stronger, and once we know where the Resistance is, we can always go back if we want, and take your family with us."

"Last time you wanted to stay with other humans, Skyler – well, need I remind you it didn't end up going too well?" I snap, gesturing to the flames around me.

Skyler doesn't miss a beat. That girl knows how to get under my skin. When my emotions blow up, she stays calm and logical and talks to me like I'm a child – *even though she's younger than me.* "We'd only have to stay there a day. We just need to throw Guardians off our path. We can stock up on supplies and then head back to Xander and your dad, ok? It's just a few more days. And we'd be a lot quicker as soon as our strength is back. While we're there, we can tell the Resistance what we learnt in Haven, to give them an advantage, *like you promised.*" She eyes me speculatively.

Now Ryder's yelling has stopped, my mind is clearer. I mumble, defeated: "If we die for them Skyler, I'll kill you."

She flashes me a knowing smile. "C'mon. When have any of my ideas been bad? Well, except the last one," she gulps, looking back toward the place we'd just escaped from. "We'll come," Skyler says, glancing at me. I reluctantly nod in agreement.

Kai smiles radiantly. Ryder turns sharply away from the group and begins to walk towards the tree line without another word.

TWENTY-FOUR

I wake with a start, my eyes snapping open. I feel groggy. I am surprised by how much of a deep sleep I've been in. I was, after all, precariously balanced on a tree branch a few hundred metres above the ground. I must have been exhausted to sleep so soundly in such an uncomfortable position. None of us stood a chance against the Mutes weakened like this, so we had decided to keep hidden as we could. Especially at night when they are more prone to attack.

The canopy of leaves above me rustles loudly and my body jerks into defence mode. A baby squirrel scampers along the branch towards me. It stops briefly to inspect me, its three bushy tails fanning out, its head cocked to one side in deliberation. *"Friend or foe?"* its eyes ask me. It decides the latter and disappears as quickly as it had come. I glance around and spot Skyler and Ryder both asleep in trees of their own.

We had trudged through the forest for hours last night, into the early hours of the morning, concealing our tracks and following Ryder's commands to perfection. Ryder had said we could rest for a few hours, but no more. Kai is the one on watch right now, I think. We'd been taking turns.

I shimmy slowly down the tree and make my way over to the lookout we had selected as the lookout area.

"How could you even think that, Leah? What is wrong with you?"

I stop in my tracks. They can't have seen me yet. I feel crappy to be listening in on a private conversation, but curiosity overcomes me. I sink closer to the tree, my shadow disappearing underneath its wide canopy.

"No. Kai, look, you don't understand. We need to save ourselves. Let's just go. Right now. You and me. We can find some place safe, and after, you know, we do what we have to do … we could be safe."

Do what we have to do?

I take a few steps closer in, careful not to alert them to my presence.

"Leah, look. I know we have some history. But I want you to understand, I don't feel the same way. I'm not just going to abandon Ava or the others. They're my friends – and you just don't do that, Leah. Where the hell is your loyalty? She saved you. Skyler almost died because of it."

"Yes, Kai, and I will always be grateful for that. But you know what Haven is like, and even the people surviving on the outside – if there are any left – well, those people are vicious. You haven't been out of Haven for a while and neither have I. We need to give ourselves the best chance we can. We have to do what we need to in order to survive."

"I can't."

A long silence.

"Is it because of her?" Leah asks.

My breath catches.

"Leah…"

"I've seen the way you look at her."

"I'm staying because it's the right thing to do. It's got nothing to do with anything else. I won't do that to them. I won't go with you."

"I thought you loved me," she murmurs. I clench my fists.

"Leah." Kai's voice is harder now, a warning.

"You said so yourself, Kai. Do you forget that you told me that, before I went to permanent testing, for you? I would have *died* for you. And now I'm trying to save us, and this is how you react."

"If you try this... You can't do it, Leah. You have to promise me. I can protect you - you don't need to do this. But if you put her in danger, Leah... I'll... I'll do what I have to do to stop you." It's quiet for a few moments as she considers the threat.

"Promise me, Leah." Kai sounds firm. What was he trying to protect me from? Leah just sounded like she wanted out, to go it alone with Kai. How does that put me in any danger?

A bizarre wave of jealousy washes through me. I had saved her and now a girl I hardly know is trying to take away the one person that kept me sane in Haven. Envy claws at my skin, infecting every pore. As far as I'm concerned, Leah leaving our group won't harm me one bit, not now that I've seen where her loyalties lie. But it's the unknowns that concern me most – I've overheard too much, but not enough.

A snap of a branch under my foot indicates they aren't alone. Without another option, I sheepishly step out from my hiding spot. Leah is huddled in Kai's arms, her face curled into his shoulder. Her head snaps around to see who the intruder is, her expression hard. Even with a tear-stained face she still looks stunning. I stand my ground unabashed, my arms folded defensively.

Leah shifts uncomfortably. She almost looks guilty. What the hell did I miss in that conversation? There seems to be more to it, but I can't figure out exactly what it is. "I'll leave you to your watch." Leah climbs down from where she has been sitting beside Kai and stalks away into the darkness.

I take a few tentative steps towards Kai, who has now also climbed down from his perch. "I'm sorry. About that. I didn't mean to—" I stop, too ashamed to continue, my eyes cast down.

"It's all good. Always thought you'd make a good spy." His lips turn up slightly as he glances toward me playfully, his previous seriousness with Leah forgotten. That smile I remember seeing when we first met, when he was healing my finger. My finger had never returned. Not yet, anyway. But I'm hoping once the serum wears off it will. That smile is there, but something's off; it doesn't reach his eyes. "How are you feeling?" Kai asks carefully.

"Better. Stronger."

"That's good. Ryder's a man on a mission at the moment, so I'm sure he'll keep us moving as soon as he wakes up."

"Yeah," I agree absently.

I look up at the large tree I am leaning against, and I wonder about how long it's been there. Before the Cull? Probably. Hundreds of years it has been alive and all this tree has done is give: oxygen, shelter, safety, beauty. I've only been alive for seventeen years and all I've done is take.

Apex's face swims into my mind.

"Do you want me to take watch for a while? You must be tired," I say.

Kai shakes his head. "Nah, I can't sleep anyway."

"Oh – ok..."

He interjects abruptly, "Did you hear what Leah and I were talking about?"

"Yes." I can't lie, not to him.

He gulps, his chin dropping to his chest and his gaze falling towards the ground. His hands dig deep into his pockets. His brow furrows in worry and panic.

"I didn't hear it all, but I think I get the gist of it. She wants to leave? Ditch the Resistance and run away. But just the two of you, right?" I mutter bitterly.

He blinks a few times, his eyes darting about as if looking for an answer. "Sort of." His breath is constricted, pained.

"What do you mean, sort of?"

"She wanted to—" He opens his mouth, as if there's more he wants to tell me and then clamps it shut again. "Yeah, um, that's what she wanted to do. Like you said. But I convinced her not to." I've never seen him like this before: so uncomfortable, slightly fragile.

"You never told me you had a thing with her, Kai."

"Would it have changed your mind to save her from permanent testing if I did?"

"Of course not." I snap.

"Anyway, it's ancient history."

A painful silence.

"You can go to sleep, honestly. I want to stay on watch." I pause as my brain returns to the moment the knife hit Apex square in the chest.

"I'll stay close," he promises.

Kai perches on a branch just above me, ready to sleep. I stay on the ground. I pick up a stick and begin to make marks in the mud below me absentmindedly. I scribble a while until I look down again. I see what I've written: 1641. My Mark. The back of my neck burns as I realize it will never come off. What happened in Haven will be with me until the day I die. Even after that, the Mark will remain.

Images of faces I'd met in Haven return to me. 821: a kind lady who had offered me help to fix a tear in my uniform. 1427: a small boy whose smile had reminded me eerily of Xander. They were all still in there. Still suffering. I hadn't given one thought to them, only my family's safety. I was so selfish.

My face is suddenly wet. "It's ok. It's ok. You're safe," I whisper to myself again and again. Even when my mind knows the truth, I try to fool it. Because it's not ok. I am not safe. Nobody is. And every bone in my body is telling me that one day, I will have to go back to Haven again.

Suddenly, a body is next to me. He must have heard the sniffs. Dammit. I hate crying in front of people. I wipe them away, feeling embarrassed.

"You don't have to do that. You don't have to be ashamed of them."

"Of what?" I counter.

Kai pulls my chin up, and I meet his eyes reluctantly. "Feeling."

I say nothing and return to my watch.

TWENTY-FIVE

I wake for the second time in a few short hours. This time, I see a face peering down toward me that looks pretty darn furious. Yet again.

"Sorry to interrupt this little rendezvous, but we need to go. Now," Ryder says.

Leah is a few steps behind Ryder, shifting from one foot to the other, arms crossed. Her breathing is rapid. Skyler is a few steps further back, smirking unapologetically. Looking around me, I get my bearings and realize I have fallen asleep, finally. And my body is sprawled across Kai's lap.

Oh.

I quickly extract my body from his, shrugging off the hand that had been placed delicately on my hair. Kai grunts as he stands up. I stare back defiantly at Ryder, trying to hide the blush that is no doubt exploding across my face. "What's up?" I ask a little breathlessly, sitting up and shuffling as far away from Kai as possible.

"We're being tracked," Ryder says.

"But how do you—? We covered all of our tracks," I protest.

"Guardians are well-trained. No time to chat about it." He chucks me a backpack, a little too hard. "Let's go."

Even after one day of no injections from the nurses, I can already see that they are all beginning to return to our natural, able-bodied states. Their reactions are that much faster, they can run that much longer. And we sure as hell are going to use it to our best advantage. We run as hard and as fast as possible. I run alongside Skyler, who keeps giving me sneaky glances, which I pointedly ignore. My breath comes in ragged gasps, and I fall behind the group. Skyler stops.

"You ok?"

I nod. "I think ... the antidote that bought me back to strength yesterday - I think there are side effects."

"Keep up," I hear Ryder order, now a few hundred metres in front of us.

"Hold my hand. I'll pull you along," Skyler says. I don't need to be told twice and her hand entwines in mine, as we launch through the forest. "Can you hear that?" she asks, her breathing still even.

"No." I gasp, even with her pulling me, I can't keep up. *Damn that antidote.*

And then I hear it too; a whirring of machines. About a kilometre or so behind us. Panic sets in and I push my legs harder. They are closing the gap between us and them, and the only weapons we have are our knives and three guns, with only a few bullets left.

It might have been minutes or hours but Ryder, who is leading our group, begins to slow and I see that we have reached the destination he intended. The trees begin to thin, indicating we are close to the edge of the forest. We arrive at the precipice of a huge cliff. Below it a river flows angrily.

"You've got to be kidding me," Skyler grunts.

"We have to. It's the only way we are going to lose them," says Ryder. "We'll never outrun their vehicles."

He's right. They sound so close. We're running out of time. No one else looks convinced.

Ryder tries another tactic: "We need to get to the Resistance's base undetected, or everyone there will be killed, too. Is that what you want?" He looks utterly sick as he recounts the reality of the situation – a reality we all know. The thin line of his lips tells us he is just as scared as we all are, but that there is no other option. If we want to see another day, this is the only way out.

Leah glances toward Kai. He ignores her, and makes his way to the edge, muttering to himself or to us – I can't be sure. "Shouldn't hurt us too bad," he says. "Would have hurt a lot more yesterday, right?"

Without another word, Ryder nods once at Kai and leaps off the edge, legs flailing in the air, his body already attempting to find the right position he needs to soften the fall. Leah follows shortly after and Kai throws me one last glance before jumping himself.

Skyler and I are the only ones who remain. I glance at her to check she's alright. She's always hated heights. She sighs rather dramatically, resigned to her fate.

"We go together, on three, ok?" I say.

Skyler nods quickly. I grasp her hand, guiding us to the edge of the rocks.

"One... Two..."

A growl of an engine erupts behind us, and before I have time to register what is happening, machines burst from the bushes, firing at us with the biggest guns I've seen yet. The sound is deafening.

I push Skyler off the cliff but I stand my ground, extricating my hand from her own, despite the bullets that seem to be coming closer to their target. My body blocks hers so they can't touch her as she falls.

I bring my own gun up quickly, settling it in the position Ryder has taught me, and freeze as I see the man a few metres beyond the barrel of my rifle. White Suit's face appears in the blur of movement around me, and contorts in rage and fury, and ... something else. Something almost ... is it relief?

Whatever it is, it terrifies me.

I can't seem to recall how to move.

The world slows and speeds at the same time as I feel my foot slip from underneath me. I hear a sharp intake of breath – mine or his?

The cliff, sure and still, seems to mock my poor luck as I tumble backwards helplessly, the gun flying out of my hand.

I see White Suit's features contort in panic, his eyes bulging as he reaches out for me in vain – but he is too far away and I am falling too fast.

I plummet towards the churning water below. But I am not ready. I'm not prepared for the fall and my unwilling body will not adjust to the shape I need it to become to fall safely.

Time seems to hold itself stagnant as I fall through the air. All too soon I am nearing the river, and without being able to manoeuvre my body into the right position I hit the water with my back.

Hard.

Is this a road? Concrete? Not water at all, I think. Not water. Something harder than water. Something solid.

But soon enough the concrete feel gives way and my breath sticks in my throat as I sink into the roiling current.

Not solid at all: moving, boiling, tugging.

I fight hard against my traitorous ribs, willing them to expand by gasping but no air returns to me.

The current is so strong I am sucked further again into the flow of the river, forced underneath the water. My whole body aches for the oxygen the river so cruelly denies me.

I wait for the adapts to kick in. For my body to save me.

But this time, it doesn't.

I can't move.

I can't breathe.

A small hand descends through the water and grabs the front of my top, yanking me up. As I break the water's now fully fluid surface, I gasp in sweet and piercing cold air.

Skyler pulls me up onto her chest as she floats face up, cradling me gently, careful to keep my head out of the water. We drift further along down the river.

"Hold on to me," she says.

Safe in Skyler's arms, I stare up to the cliffs. Surrendering to the torrent that surrounds us, Skyler turns her body towards the cliff, holding me in front of her, shoving me forward so she'll be exposed to gunfire. She is protecting me. And she's doing it well.

A dark figure looks on as we round the river's corner. I can just make out his hand in the air as if giving a command, and then he disappears out of sight. I only glimpse him for a couple seconds, and then he is gone.

We navigate the water as best we can, coughing and spluttering through the rough current. Skyler spots something and turns course, swimming horizontally against the current. Now we are heading towards a few familiar figures standing on the shoreline in the distance.

She half drags and half carries me towards land. I help as best I can. Suddenly Kai and Ryder are there, each on either side of my body, my arms around their shoulders. They lift me quickly out of the water and pull me onto the rocks.

Skyler collapses in a shallow spot by the river's edge. She puffs manically from the exertion. "Thanks for the help guys," I hear her laugh bitterly.

As I turn around trying to breathe out a thank you to her, Ryder hushes me. "She's fine. Just keep breathing. You've been winded badly. Kai, it's fine," he snaps. "I've got her."

Ryder half snatches me from Kai's grasp and cradles me in his own, carefully setting me down on a large rock. He coaches me on breathing: all the way in and then all the way out, his calm voice soothing my panic. His hands run over my body checking for other injuries. When my breathing normalizes, he doesn't miss a beat: "We need to go," he says.

"What the hell are you talking about? She almost died!" Skyler pipes up, rounding on Ryder.

"No, no, he's right," I pant. "We don't know how long we've got." I puff. "If the Guardians come looking for us. We've got a head start for now."

Silence washes over the group as they consider Ryder's cold yet correct calculations, and my assent.

"Kai, you take the front. I'll take the back position and keep anyone from lagging behind." Ryder pointedly glances at me and I feel my lips tighten. I'm angry at the fact I'm so weak and exposed compared to everyone else. I'm seething, actually. I'm the weak link. But I know the truth too – that if we hadn't jumped we'd all be dead, or worse.

"Are you sure we're ok to go ahead, Ava? It's your call. Not his." Kai juts his chin out toward Ryder.

"Honestly. Thanks, Kai, but I'm fine."

Skyler comes to my side and indicates to Kai with a nod; I watch as he reluctantly begins hiking towards the safe canopy of the forest, indicating we should follow. I offer a weak smile to encourage him, but he just shakes his head worriedly, his lips pressed together, before turning away to take the lead.

Leah is still and silent, her arms crossed. She looks terrified. She's not much help at all, really. Leah takes one final look at me and then trots after Kai. Skyler begins to help me down but she is too short for the task – Ryder has placed me on a rock too difficult for her shorter arms to get to.

"I've got it," Ryder says. Skyler nods in agreement and heads off to join the others.

As he lifts me down from the rock, I close my eyes and breathe out. My exhalation comes in a splutter of multiple coughs. Ryder holds firm and still, until I stop shaking and wheezing. He sets me down slowly, and I am suddenly reminded of the first time we met in Haven.

The concern in his eyes. It's still there – it's just more guarded, more careful. There's a dark sense of worry on his face. I drop my hands from around his neck, and his hands disappear from my waist as quickly as they had been placed there.

I don't thank him. I stalk off after Skyler without another word.

I regret it immediately.

TWENTY-SIX

"I've changed my mind." I break the silence so violently that Ryder jumps in the air.

The deer he and I had been tracking for the past twenty minutes darts out of sight at the sound of my voice. Ryder gestures to his lost food in disbelief, looking at me in annoyance. "I almost had that deer."

"No, you didn't. Your posture was all wrong, so your aim was way off. Guns have made you sloppy."

He rolls his eyes, but I see a whisper of a smile playing on his lips. "Well, you'll just have to take the lead. After you." He makes a grandiose gesture as if I were a queen about to enter her court.

I ignore the quip and point deeper into the forest. "There are more tracks over there." We begin the hunt again.

"Ok, what have you been thinking about so hard that it was worth losing our dinner over?"

I turn to him. This is something I'd been thinking about since killing Axel. How good it felt to make someone pay for the suffering they've caused. "Revenge. I want even. I want to help the Resistance take down the Chosen. I just... I can't stop thinking about the people still in there. Still suffering. I can't stand by and let them do that to people. It makes me as bad as them. *Worse* than them."

He stops in his tracks. "Well, that definitely was worth losing dinner over. If we have you on our side, we could just about stage the attack on Haven with just you and I." His eyes gleam. "When your adapts are back to normal, of course."

"Yes, but my family comes first. I need to make sure they are safe. That needs to be my priority."

"Of course."

"And Skyler, when the attack goes down on Haven, she can't be anywhere near."

"I think you'll have to deal with that one yourself," he says carefully, "you two aren't ones to be told what to do – Marked or not."

"Ryder..." Something else had been playing on my mind on our journey, but I hadn't felt like I could say anything. I don't like to worry or fret. It's weakness. And I don't like people to see or hear me do it, either. But I find myself saying it to him. I don't know why.

"What—what if ... what if my adapts never come back? What if that serum I took before we escaped ... what if it was an experiment and it was a failure? What if I'm stuck like this? How am I going to help anybody then?"

His expression grows grim as he takes a step toward me. He's battling with how to say this. I brace for the worst. "Ave..." He's never called me that before. "The Chosen didn't tell Guardians much, but what I do know is that serum was the best they'd come up with yet, to make themselves like us. As Skyler had figured out. I couldn't risk telling you anything or helping you in Haven. I think he suspected ... well, there were always eyes on me. I didn't want to put any of you in danger. But that particular serum she found? Every Chosen he'd tested it out on ... they died."

"Died?" My voice rises an octave.

"Yes... But they didn't have any adapts at all before he gave them the serum. They were as weak as the Marked. They received adapts for about a day ... none as advanced as yours are though, and then they caught a fever and, um, died. I'm not going to lie to you, Ava." He runs a hand through his hair as he searches for the right words to say. "It was risky what you did in Haven. Really risky. But it paid off. I guess you've just gotta ask yourself... If you were in that position again, would you do it?" His eyes trail the floor as he speaks, each word he says sounds like a strain. "I've done things I'm not proud of, but put in the situation again – if it meant I am standing here right now, with you ... a potential weapon against *him*..." We both knew who he was referring to.

"Yeah, I'd do it again."

I think about that day. If I hadn't made that decision. I'd still be in there. Skyler might be dead by now. They might have learned where my family was and brought them to Haven. Kai would still be in there. "I'd do it again," I nod.

"Then, that sacrifice was worth it."

I suddenly realize how close I am standing to him. How he is just one head taller than me exactly. We look at each other for a moment, examining. The stillness is nice. There's heat in his eyes. Looking at him like this ... it feels dangerous. Like we are both about to explode. I feel the danger in him, the darkness that he tries to hide, and I don't look away. I have no doubt he sees the same thing in my own eyes. We've both lost so much. But right here, looking at him, I finally feel like someone understands.

A small cough comes from behind us and we both jump apart wildly, knives in our hands ready to fight whoever is there.

A stranger.

I push Ryder behind me, knives poised to be thrown.

Is he a Guardian? Has White Suit found us already? A wide smile emerges from his lips and my heart sinks.

Ryder relaxes his gun, a whisper of a smile playing on his mouth.

"Ryder," the stranger acknowledges coolly. "I see you've been productive with your time undercover." He gestures to where I'm standing.

The stranger smirks at me, pleased with his own wit.

"Jayden," Ryder breathes, then turns to me. "Ava, meet my little brother."

TWENTY-SEVEN

Jayden bounds over to Ryder and knocks into him with such force that I think they might wind each other. "You have no idea how much I've missed you!" Ryder beams at him with the warmth of the sun.

"You must be Ava, then." His grin is wide. "Ryder got a message to me. Told me all about you. That you could help us take them down."

"Oh, did he, now." I glare at him. It wasn't until five minutes ago that I'd agreed in full to join the Resistance after I'd got my family back. He must have known I'd come around in the end, I guess. I turn to Ryder who looks sheepishly at me and shrugs.

"Where's Thomas? How long ago did you guys escape? That hasn't happened since we did it!"

Since they did it? Since they broke out of Haven?

I shoot him a sideways glance, so many questions in my eyes.

"Story for another day," he mumbles.

Jayden laughs but confusion is evident in his expression. "Where's Thomas? I thought we agreed you'd infiltrate from the inside until we were ready to take Haven? You'd both help us from undercover? Help us get in? Why was that plan abandoned? I haven't heard from you since you sent the message about Ava."

Ryder's expression is sombre as he meets his little brother's eyes and shakes his head slowly. Jayden's face drops; something clicks into place in his brain, and his expression turns into a grimace. "Shit." He punches the tree.

Well, at least I can discern one thing from this conversation: *his* strength has definitely not been altered by injections. Splinters fly, and when he pulls his fist away, the trunk of the hundred-year-old tree shows a gaping hole in it. He throws another punch and I see the tree shake, almost snapping in half. Thomas, the man Ryder said was like a father to him, who raised him.

I glance at Ryder, but he has all eyes on Jayden, his expression unreadable. "How?" Jayden's head hangs low.

"He was the closest thing we had to a father. He was the only family we had left." I see tears well in Jayden's eyes, but he refuses to let them fall.

Ryder says softly, "I wanted to wait. To tell you in person. He went out well, Jayden. When it all went down ... well, he died with courage. And for a good cause. *Our* cause." Ryder steps closer, placing a hand on Jayden's shoulder. "You've still got me. We're going to make them pay for everything they've done, I swear it."

Jayden nods and then seems to internally shake himself. His tone is clipped and removed, reminding me all too well of his older brother. I can see the resemblance. Jayden can't be more than two years younger than him. Probably my age, actually.

"Well, it's good to have you back – it's been a while. We need as much information as you all collected in there. Information about Haven: its layout, its armoury, and defence information."

"We can help with that," Ryder confirms.

Jayden continues: "I think a few more numbers to our ranks is essential before we attack. We have been trying to recruit but nowadays it's getting harder and harder to find others without Mutes or Chosen getting to them first. The number of deserted camps we've found… But I still reckon in a few months we will be ready to make our attack."

"I don't think we have that long," I say. Jayden's sharp eyes turn to me.

"Why not?" he asks.

"The Doctor's after the Resistance," Ryder says. "More than ever before."

TWENTY-EIGHT

"I mean, it's not in the shape it used to be that's for sure. Some people left. When Thomas wasn't here anymore, a lot of people got spooked and just ditched."

We'd been walking for a few hours now, once we'd caught up Leah, Kai, and Skyler on the situation at hand. Jayden led us to a track up into the mountains, so we needed minimal time to cover our tracks now. I'd been quizzing Jayden on the Resistance for the past hour. Ryder falls into step with us both.

Up ahead, Leah and Kai are walking and speaking quietly to each other. There seems to be some sort of tension between them. Kai furtively keeps glancing behind to where Ryder, Jayden, and I walk. Skyler has volunteered to take the rear, cover tracks, and is listening out for potential threats. Mutes and Chosen alike.

I can feel my strength and speed slowly returning, but as for my special adapts – none had surfaced. They all walked at the pace I needed them to, as I still wasn't back to full strength. To say it infuriates me would be the understatement of the century. "So, Thomas wasn't your dad? Was he with your mum?"

The question was to both of them but Ryder answered: "Nah. I don't remember a lot about my dad at all. Just images. Pretty good-looking though." He throws a sideways grin at me and I look back at him incredulously.

I like this side of Ryder: he seems lighter, now he's back with his brother. But as he talks about his parents his sombre expression returns. "We got captured when I was about four. Haven was newer, not as fortified as it is now. She sacrificed herself for us. Mum. She knew that with Thomas we would be in the right hands. He taught me everything I know." He talks softly, so softly I have to lean in to hear him over the crunching of our feet on the dry forest floor.

"How did Thomas die, Ryder?"

"I told you. The Doctor killed him." I feel I have pushed too much. Whatever had happened to Thomas, Ryder doesn't want to revisit it. The darkness is back again and I find myself wishing I'd never asked.

"When my mum died, I felt like I was just making everything up as I went along," I say. "I had to look after my family because my dad no longer could. He got injured from the Mute that killed my mum. He barely made it out alive. From that moment on, it was my responsibility to keep them alive." I grimace at the thought, "It still is."

"Eldest children, eh?" he says, pushing Jayden playfully. "The weight of the world on our shoulders." Jayden smirks at Ryder and then hangs back to take Skyler's position.

I feel like I suddenly understand why Ryder was so emotionless once we had broken free from Haven. He was doing everything he could to get back to his brother. Xander's laugh echoes in my mind. A tidal wave of guilt washes over me. I need to get back to them. As soon as possible. "How long is it to the Resistance?"

"Few more hours," he replies.

I smile at Ryder and he returns it tentatively.

"Just wait until they see you." He chuckles as if he knows what's to come.

And for the first time, in a long time, I'm excited to see what's next, too.

TWENTY-NINE

One hundred pairs of eyes and thirty loaded guns stare menacingly at us as we step into the Resistance base. Skyler feels me shift beside her. She runs her hand along mine in comfort and nods. *It will be ok,* her eyes tell me.

The hall is dark: most of the windows have been boarded up with wooden planks. Light seeps through in small cracks but I blink several times as my eyes adjust. A podium made of wooden boxes is at the front of the room, and it seems to be where Ryder is making his way, so I fall into step behind him. I scan the scene for the nearest escape route and notice several entries to this central space, opening out to different corridors. I begin to panic at the thought of being unable to find my way out of this building. I see a flash of my cell back at Haven and shiver slightly. I shuffle closer to the boarded window and some peace enters my mind as I feel a ray of sun on my cheek.

At the front of the large hall where everyone is gathered, Jayden is already calming the crowd, asking for their attention, climbing onto the wooden boxes. He seems calm and in control. I am impressed and wait with the rest of the crowd, to hear what he'll say. "These guys are with us," he says, pointing to us. "They escaped from Haven. Which hasn't happened since I managed to do it, and they've completed their task alongside none other than the man I did it with." There is a lull and I can tell Jayden is relishing the moment. He says, loudly to the crowd, "Ryder, my brother, is back."

A few people reach out and touch Ryder's shoulder in excitement and support. He looks back to the crowd impassively. Not many notice the darkness there, his grief for Thomas, like I do. Many eyes in the room are glued hungrily on Ryder and Kai equally. I swallow and look away quickly.

While Ryder and Jayden have moved to the front, Kai, Skyler and I stay where we are; with Leah tentatively peering out from behind Kai. A small girl about Xander's age pokes her head out from behind her mother's leg to look at our group. I catch her eye and give her a small smile, but her eyes go wide in horror and she retreats back behind her mother.

An older woman speaks up: "Don't be ridiculous," she says. "No one has done that in years." Grey peppers her mousy brown hair piled in a bun on her head. Her frown lines are etched deeply between her brows. She is built incredibly: arms sculpted and shoulders broad. "And how can we trust them?" she continues. "Don't prisoners get their heads shaved? What about that one? How come she hasn't?" She points to me and I have the sudden urge to curl up into a ball and avoid eye contact. I grip to the remnants of my courage and stare back defiantly.

"The Doctor has taken a ... liking to her," offers Jayden. "I can't tell you much right now, but he did tests on her, because she's special. I won't say any more than that for now."

In case my adapts never come back, and you don't give these people false hope that I'm this super weapon come to save them.

I gulp.

"Don't judge her too harshly – after all, she's the one who busted these guys out." I notice a look of playful amusement dance across Jayden's sharp features as he speaks. Jayden has learned the whole story from Ryder. The journey back here provided plenty of time for the brothers to catch up on the relevant information. He told him of my trouble-making escapades in my time at Haven, but also of the strange rules White Suit had begun to put into action after I'd arrived there. All of which I was unaware of at the time.

There had always been a Guardian on watch specifically for me. They were never allowed to be more than a few metres away. Ryder had been Chosen as the main Guardian allocated to me, I learned on the journey. No doubt that was the reason why he always seemed to be around to stop me before I did something stupid.

It was strange to hear someone else talk about me in this way, to see the movements around me from someone else's point of view. Every part of Haven was locked down in some way, you need a key card to access almost everything. I realize just how crazy our escapade had been and how impossible it would have been if I hadn't had the antidote in my system, with a Guardian on our side.

After I'd heard White Suit's overprotective rules for me I had shivered in disgust and ... something else. Intrigue?

I wish you to be comfortable until the time is right, Ava. That's what White Suit had said. The time is right. The time is right for *what?* Why was I being kept alive? Was there more to my protection than I realized? Why did he want me to never be alone? Was he afraid I was a threat? Or was it something else?

Another girl bounds our way, catching Ryder's arm. She pouts, looking to him and Jayden as she asks, "How do we know she's not one of them? She could be an undercover agent for them – like you were, Ryder."

"She's not."

Another older woman speaks: "But how do we know to trust her? My children are here. I need to know I can protect them. I don't know her."

"I said, she's not working with them." Ryder's voice echoes through the hall harsh and cold. He recovers quickly as he scans his audience, sensing he is losing the crowd. The group hums with murmurs. There is clearly dissent.

I thought this was going to be a fit fighting force, ready to take back their people, and save the others in Haven, ready to triumph over their oppressors. I'd imagined a Resistance many times since I first heard of them several weeks before. I look around now, at the crowd we've come to. A lot of these *fighters* are mothers with a few young children clutching at their legs. An older man stands watching us with a walking stick. I notice the few able-bodied young men and women have shuffled their way to the front in protection mode, but they have an air of uncertainty, of weakness.

The Resistance looks tired and small. I can see exhaustion creeping in on the older members' faces. I can see curiosity and anxiety in the younger ones. But really, the main thing I see is fear. Fear of the unknown. Fear of me. This doesn't look like an army ready to take down the Chosen to me.

"Ava is one of us. You'll have to trust me," says Ryder, again raising his voice to the crowd. "Anyone who has a problem with her can talk to me."

"And me." Another voice echoes and strengthens what Ryder has just said. I am shocked to see Jayden come to my defence so quickly without knowing me. How does he know he can trust me? I guess he's not sticking up for me alone: he is standing with his brother, united in their leadership of the group.

But it's not going to be enough. I can see their stares of distrust. I have to win over this crowd on my own. "Ryder, I understand where she's coming from." Ryder looks at me with worry, probably scared I'm about to ruin his plan to protect me. I stride past him and stand in front of the group, next to Jayden. I step up to the wooden podium. "I have trouble having faith in others, too. I've seen my fair share of idiots, enough to know never to live with a bunch of 'em." I crack a smile.

Sullen faces. I move on swiftly.

"This world is ruthless. If we want to survive, we have to fight like hell to make it happen. That's what I've been doing for the past seventeen years of my life."

I pause to gauge a reaction. There are no protests, so I blunder on, my nerves taut.

"And if you think for one second that any of those behind me, any of my group, would do anything to hurt you – well you're right."

Gasps come from around the group.

"These people behind me, they have been my family in Haven. And beyond. Kai and Skyler, they've both saved my life on different occasions. And Leah, endured hell in permanent testing."

Leah stands a little taller. Kai nods to me in encouragement. My nerves are no longer fraying.

"And if you did anything to harm me, they would not hesitate to take you down. And the same goes the other way. You can bet on it. But don't you see? That's exactly what White... the Doctor, the Chosen, the Guardians ...That is exactly what they've made of me. We are stronger because they tried to oppress us. They've given me strength. And unlike them, we have something to fight for. They... they tortured me." I gulp.

"And they almost killed the girl I consider to be my sister."

Skyler nods solemnly.

"And they tried to kill Leah, Kai, and Ryder. My—" I look at their faces and clear my throat before glancing back. "My ... friends. We took what was ours – our freedom ... but they wanted my own family to go into their torture. Their experiments. The same way they want your families in there too."

There are whispers in the crowd. And then silence, waiting for more.

I continue: "Well, no more. We need to free those people in there. And we need to free ourselves. We cannot live in fear of being taken against our own will. We need to fight."

And now I'm met with silence. I make a beeline to stand beside Skyler. I add, as I go, "I'm Ava. And I'm going to fight like hell to get those people out of there. Regardless of whether you trust me or not."

When we left Haven, I wanted to head back to my family and never set eyes on the Resistance again. And now I'm swearing to fight alongside them. Allegiance is a strange thing. And, I need them to trust me. Skyler's right: if I wanted certainty my family was always going to be safe from the Chosen, we needed to take them down ourselves.

Those around me seem to look convinced and the older woman nods solemnly before stepping back into the crowd. There is no overwhelming sense that I've swayed them, but I don't feel stares of mistrust anymore, either.

Jayden steps up to speak again. "Well, with that sorted, welcome to the Resistance, Ava, Skyler, Kai and Leah. Get back to your posts, soldiers. I want three more people on Mute-watch tonight; it's been a little quiet on that front lately. Who's on food?"

And with that, the room springs into activity and I am forgotten, except for a few apprehensive stares. Ryder saunters up and chucks me a strange-looking object, biting into one himself. "What's that?" I ask.

"A potato," he says. "Eat, you'll need your strength." He stares at me for a second longer than he should. And then he is gone, the throng of the crowd taking him to another room.

Jayden walks to my side and whispers devilishly. "You've certainly made an impact. He's a pretty hard one to crack. That potato? Savour it. That's the most caring thing I've seen him do for anyone other than me in years." He chuckles and follows quickly after Ryder.

I throw the potato up in the air and catch it before making my way down one of the corridors. Time to figure out how this place works, I guess.

THIRTY

"You know, I never thanked you properly," Leah concedes.

"Don't mention it."

Tonight, I'm on guard duty with Leah. We have been sitting together on the rooftop of the Observatory, the Resistance's base, for the past two hours, watching for potential threats. Not that she'd be much use in a fight, really. She's the timidest human I've ever met. Even the way she speaks is so soft, I have to lean in to hear her. I can't blame her for it though – who knows what she was put through in permanent testing. It would change anyone.

The Carter Observatory is one of the few buildings I've seen still fully intact. Up in the hills of Wellington – I know it's called that because I saw a sign once – on my way into this city for a hunt. It's been demolished since then, the words unrecognizable, but I used to savour the sound of the long-forgotten city, what once was, on my tongue at night before I fell asleep.

The coastline is speckled with buildings that look like they are half eaten, as if a giant has taken a huge bite out of each and every one of them. From here I would say we were only two days' walk from Haven. It's hard to believe that the escape was only two days ago. So much has happened since then.

I look down at the building we are sitting on and see if I can imagine what is happening down below us. The building itself is larger than I expected, with secret hallways and rooms opening up in all directions. Every time I look around, I make a small but wonderful discovery. My favourite room is the library: hundreds upon hundreds of books about different planets and stars and the astronauts who explored them. The room is filled with pages about things I can only imagine. The sheer enormity of the information humans had the ability to possess before the Cull scares me: the way they explored, the way they dreamed, the way they harnessed energy and creativity. It makes me feel small.

Today, Leah, Skyler, and I received yet another class of physical training and 'learning' how to fight. Even though I'd begged to differ with the instructor, I was put into the women's classes because the men were more 'advanced' in their training. Even though, adapts aside, I could kick their asses.

On the whole, my assessment was that the majority of these supposed 'soldiers' were pretty damn useless. The Resistance has been too sheltered, too pampered. Most women have been asked by Jayden to stay in the Observatory's grounds for safety, which means they have to rely on the men to go and hunt. This is a good enough division of labour – their job primarily being to stay and keep watch of the building – but it creates too many imbalances for my liking. The women are not being trained properly, and if we want to win this war, we *all* have to fight.

Within the first few minutes of our 'training' session, I'd schooled them all, and as a result was told I wasn't fighting 'fair' and was instructed by Tex, the old teacher that was still teaching them tricks for toddlers, to sit out the next round. Were they *kidding?* Since when is fighting ever going to be fair? *"Oh, sorry, one second, let me wait until you look directly at me so I can attack you."* Otherwise I'm not 'fighting fair'. *Seriously?*

Jayden had spent a good part of the first evening we'd arrived grilling us for any further information we might have on the Chosen. Details we may not have even realized we knew; things they could have overlooked, for the attack. They were thorough in the way they went about interviewing us – they viewed any new information as valuable information. They then asked if we wanted to join the training, which Skyler and I both agreed to, just to keep our skills up. My injuries and that antidote I'd taken were still weakening me. And despite the fact my fighting ability is way above anything else anyone could achieve in here, I knew that if I left right now and met a Mute, or a group of Guardians, I wouldn't be able to protect myself. So, I'm gathering my strength, and praying it'll come back soon.

Stick to the tracks I showed you, collect water from the river, and never go out at night.

I pray my eight-year-old brother would have the sense to listen to me. And Dad's there to make sure he follows instructions.

"I'm serious. Ava, I'd be dead without you. Thank you." Leah smiles tenderly in response, her eyes searching through the night's blinding darkness.

"Can I ask you something?" I say.

"Sure."

"What... What was it like? Permanent testing?" I feel her stiffen beside me. "You don't have to explain if you don't want to." I rush to retract my question. "I guess, I just want to be more informed about what we're fighting against." We are both quiet for a moment, our breath the only sound for miles.

She finally speaks: "It was awful, but worth it. I'd do it again. For him. For Kai."

Now it's my turn to stiffen. "I have people I'd do it for, too," I say. "My family. Xander, my little brother – he's only eight. And my dad."

Leah's gaze is intense as she looks at me, with a deep sense of understanding. Her voice is quiet. "Why don't you go back to them? Your family."

I sigh, my head tilting to the side slightly in indignation. It was innocent enough but I can hear the slight twinge of hope in her tone. She wants me gone. I think back to that conversation I overheard her and Kai having in the forest.

It's because of her, isn't it?

"I can't," I say. "Not yet. Ryder was right; I'm not strong enough. And I gave White Suit a complete opposite location to where my family actually are when he tortured me. I can't afford to lead him to it. If he follows our tracks here, at least I can fight. I won't risk them being found and being taken to Haven. They wouldn't last a day there. I taught my brother the basics. He'll be able to feed himself and Dad for a few weeks. But I can't help but worry he's going to run into a Mute. It's all I can think about sometimes."

She nods in agreement. It's actually nice to talk to a girl my age, get my head straight with exactly where I'm at. To know I am doing the right thing by my family, even though I can't be with them at the moment.

My shoulders relax slightly, the burden a little lighter, at least for now.

"It's actually south from Haven, not north, about two days' walk. I found a cave inside a cliff. That's where they are – my family. How amazing is that?" I smile and Leah nods in appreciation.

"The height would make it safe enough to be away from Mutes and conceal yourself from other humans you don't want to find you. Smart," she agrees.

"We've lived there ever since my mum died. It was called Eastbourne before the Cull. I like it there." I point at where my home lies, straight across Wellington harbour. I feel lost without them, and a wave of sadness overcomes me, knocking the breath from me.

I brace the subject that's both on our minds. "Are you and Kai...?"

"We're not really speaking at the moment. We had a disagreement. He—he said I'm a coward." Tears well up in her eyes.

"I'm sorry to hear that."

"So am I." She sniffs.

"You're not, by the way," I say, "He doesn't know what you went through. Someone told me once that sometimes, bravery is just surviving. No matter what horror you've had to endure, to keep going, to keep living - *that* is brave."

We look towards the stars in silence. She takes a big sigh. It sounds a lot like relief.

THIRTY-ONE

"What are you doing?" Skyler asks.

I almost jump out of my skin at her proximity. I hadn't even noticed her coming into the dorm room. I silently scold myself for not being more on guard. We're still in danger here. I need to remember that. Or I'll get soft, like these people. My bed is unmade with piles of supplies scattered on it. I am trying to decide what to take with me. "I'm packing," I grunt as I throw more supplies in the bag I've commandeered from some unsuspecting lady in the hall of the Observatory.

"For what?"

"To go home. You're coming with me."

Since spending last night on watch with Leah, my resolve had slowly dwindled. Everywhere I turn and see a child's face, I see Xander. Every time I see an older man, I hold my breath in hope that it's Dad. I have to leave. I cannot help the Resistance a moment longer without knowing the location of Xander and Dad, no matter what physical state I'm in.

Skyler shoots me a fierce look and sighs loudly, launching herself onto my bed. She locks her fingers behind her head and forces indifference by closing her eyes. "Dude," she says in an overly relaxed tone. "You can go, have fun in the cave by your lonesome. But I'm not leaving."

I turn to her. "Dude? What does that even mean?"

Skyler shrugs. "Dunno. Someone said it today. This is what I'm saying. These guys seem to know stuff, Ava. They could teach us, help us."

"More like we could help them," I say, an eyebrow raised.

"You're really going to leave and go home to your family? Leaving all of these people about to stage an attack without even giving them even a little bit of training?" she asks incredulously.

"Oh, don't pretend you're doing this for other people, Skyler. I know you. Don't think I've not noticed you sneaking off every five minutes you get to spend time with a certain someone."

Since we'd arrived, Skyler had been spending a *significant* amount of time with another fifteen-year-old – Lucy. A very beautiful fifteen-year-old. I'd seen them giggling together, sneaking longing looks at meals when they thought nobody was looking. She must think I'm stupid.

"That's not true," she scoffs, but her eyes dart around nervously. I know I've got her. She ignores my quip and soldiers on with her case: "Your strength hasn't finished returning to you since the injections. You're still weaker than you should be going into the wild. You're really going to go out there..." she gestures to the forest below, "...not on form? And by yourself? For what?"

"My family," I whisper. "We need to leave. Every day I spend here... It's driving me crazy. I don't know whether they are alive or dead, whether they are safe or if White Suit..." I gulp. "It's torturing me, Sky. I can't stand not knowing where they are. I don't feel safe here. There's something wrong here. I don't know what. All I know is I need to leave."

I know deep down she is right. I would barely be able to protect myself against a Mute. Let alone anyone else. For some reason it has taken me longer to recover from the injections than the rest of our group. Which naturally infuriates me.

"They won't be dead, I know your dad well enough that he wouldn't let that happen in a million years, even with his disability. He would have hunted with Xander, or been on guard for Mutes."

My heartbeat increases at the mere thought of it.

"You need your strength. These people need you. You promised Kai and Ryder to help these people. Think about the Marked. They need you, too. What's a few more days away? And if you wait just a couple more days," She sighs. "I'll ditch the Resistance and come with you too. You're more important to me than revenge on that lowlife that kept us locked up in there. And Lucy." She smiles, but it doesn't touch her eyes.

"You promise?" I ask her.

If I agree to Skyler's bargain, then I could get the best of both worlds. I'd be able to give the Resistance a better shot of winning against the Chosen, I'd get back to Xander, and I would be keeping Skyler out of the fighting. And she has a point about the strength thing. I would be better off on top form.

She nods furiously. "Two more days. And then we leave." She smiles triumphantly and bounds out the door.

I lie on the bed and think through the next two days: more time to train, yes. These people need that. More time to regain my strength. I need to feel better before setting out for home. There's no telling what I'll find when I leave here – not just Mutes but armies of Guardians scouring the countryside.

More time with Ryder and Kai, too.

THIRTY-TWO

The following days at the Carter Observatory are spent balancing in between discomfort and calm. And it's not just my own – everyone else's, too.

I can tell the residents or soldiers or whatever they should be called – I can't make up my mind – are still uncomfortable with my presence. So, I've taken it upon myself to prove how much of a worthy bet I am.

I move from one station to another: food preparation, look-out, nursery. I am surprised by the number of children – only three – who reside with the Resistance. I wonder why there are not more. Then I remember how difficult it had been for my mother and father to protect us when we were younger against the Mutes; to find a safe place for us to grow up. And not everyone would be able to protect their children the way my parents had. They were fierce fighters, trained only by the best, my grandfather, who had been a soldier himself.

The trivial chores bore me all too soon. I am exasperated and restless. I can't stay indoors a moment longer. I beg Ryder to let me in on a strategy meeting or go hunting for the group.

He denies me, of course. "No can do, babe." He glances at me with the devil in his eyes as he says that last word.

"What is this, 'babe'? What do these things mean ... 'babe'?" I ask incredulously, squinting my eyes at him at the foreign word.

"It's a term of endearment." He laughs. "But no, you can't. A team of hunters have already been sent out today – Leah went with them. She asked first." He sees how I want to cut in and adds, "And you aren't trusted enough to be in the strategy room, yet. Sorry." He shrugs and jogs off as he sees Jayden across the hall, talking animatedly with a few of the men.

I stalk off, heading outside. I stomp in the direction of the vegetable garden, a hundred metres from the Observatory grounds. It was here just yesterday, when I met a woman named Sarah. She showed me the large patch of tilled soil, proud to share the fruits of her labour, which included the moat she had dug around the garden so no rabbits could get to it without a nasty surprise coming their way. I gulped at the similarity of the moat around most of Haven. My mind travels back to that man's screams...

I shake my head hard and try to think of easier things. I find myself thinking that it would be nice to have a vegetable plot back near our cave. When I get back. We could plant it together, Skyler, Xander and I. Desperate to do something with my hands that requires at least some physical exertion, I make my way over to the garden, jumping the moat, and begin to dig holes to plant more of those stupid potatoes everyone seems to love. They are actually pretty good, I concede – if only to myself.

"Hey stranger." I look up to see Kai standing there, hands in his pockets as he admires my work.

"Hi," I huff back, continuing my work.

"You alright?" he asks.

"Just itchy feet. You could come help if you wanted? Make yourself useful." I grin up at him from my furious digging, wiping the beads of sweat off my forehead. I lean down and chuck him an abandoned spade next to me.

A smile flickers on his face as he catches it and kneels down to begin digging beside me. "Not used to spending this much time in one place?" he says.

"It's not that. We would spend days at a time back at the cave. I think, I just... I want to be more helpful here, make a difference a little while I'm still around. Ryder won't let me into strategy meetings yet and Jayden hasn't followed up on his promise for me to go out hunting with a group. There are so many rules here. I don't like it."

I remember Ryder telling me I must follow the rules, out of respect for the system they had going here. They all seemed so trivial to me. I seem to spend most of my life lined up these days. They line up in a single file every meal, line up for the shower, line up to use this thing they call a toilet. Why couldn't I just go in a bush like normal people do?

He considers that for a moment, staring at the army of trees a few metres away from where we are digging. "I think you unsettle people."

"Yeah, well, for one, speaking of rules..." I see him hesitate, but then he continues. "The Doctor bent his rules for you, which is weird. You've told us that you believe he wants you for something. His grand plan or whatever. And now you've escaped, the scouts have reported that there are hundreds more Guardian patrols for miles around. People are wondering what he wants with you. Or what you want with us."

His expression is neutral but I can see a hint of worry in his eyes, grinding away at him. That little grain of doubt. It's there, even in Kai, haunting him. I can see him wondering, too; am I a traitor?

The tattoo engraved on the back of my neck tingles and I reach up to run my fingers along it. Kai sits up, takes his spade and starts digging again. We keep silent as we continue to dig, not daring to look at once another. I am pained by his doubt, but it's understandable.

Carefully placing the words into the potato patch below us, not daring to look at me or say it too loud I hear, "You know, I'm glad you didn't leave just yet."

I look up abruptly. "How did you know I was planning on leaving?" I roll my eyes as I connect the dots all too quickly. That meddling little...

"Skyler." His eyes avert from mine, his feet shuffling on the ground a little.

He sees my annoyance and adds, a little feebly: "I didn't mean to – I was coming to talk to you about ... about, well never mind. And I bumped into Skyler and we got talking and..."

I don't respond and instead, look across the ocean to the cliffs where my family reside.

Hold on, Xander, I'll be there soon.

"I'm sorry I didn't tell you. I just thought leaving would be less difficult. You know, if I didn't." I mumble. My eyes touch the sky for a few moments; now it's my turn to avoid his gaze. When I finally return Kai's stare I feel a small flutter in my stomach.

I think back to when we met in Haven, how I saved him, how he'd pulled me from my darkest moments, the escape – and I finally understand the worry, the darkness in his eyes. It's pain.

"You didn't bother to let me know? You didn't think I'd want to come, maybe?"

"I..." No words come to me.

I didn't realize to what extent this would actually hurt Kai. After years of not having many relationships or ties to anyone but my family, I seem to have too many to look after these days. I'm so bad at this.

He gently reaches out a hand and traces it down my cheek, freeing the hair that the wind has blown there. He tucks it behind my ear. The tension of the movement, the meaning... My breath quickens. Our eyes lock. I see the longing in his, the heat there. He cups my face in his hands.

I take a step back from him.

I can't do this. I won't go down this road with him. He'd been the only thing that had held me here, to this earth, to sanity in Haven. He's been my best friend. And if I don't move away now, everything will change between us. Maybe for the worse. And I won't risk losing him. I know him so well now, it's almost as he sees the thoughts crossing through my mind.

He changes tack: "I want to come with you when you leave."

"But what about the Resistance?" I counter. "Don't you want to hurt the people that hurt us? That killed your mum?"

"Don't *you*?" His voice has risen and I am shocked to see a slight resentment flash across his face. What is his *problem*? The boy was trying to kiss me two seconds ago.

"Why don't you want to fight with us? I don't get it, Ava. You can't say one thing and then do another." He spits the words at me, knowing they will land hard. Knowing my insecurities like I know his own.

I say simply and assertively, "You can't trust anyone but your own blood. I'm backing mine. I made a promise and I intend to keep it."

"But you can. What about me? What about us?" I feel exasperated with his confusing comments. And I find myself pulling away from his touch.

"What even does that mean, Kai? Who's 'us'? You? The Resistance? I barely know these people. I barely know you." My heart plummets as I see how much that has hurt him. "Kai – I'm so sorry, I didn't—"

Ryder's pointed cough comes from behind, and we spin around in a fury.

"What!?" we both say in unison, furious.

"Jayden has organized for the women to be taught by you, now. They are all waiting on the field for fight training," Ryder says. His eyes are light and amused, as if he's happy someone else is on the receiving end of my fury for once.

I scowl and storm off, gaining distance from Kai in seconds, with Ryder in hot pursuit. "You do seem to have a talent for pissing people off, Ava," he says, a smile in his voice. We are walking towards the group of women waiting in a clearing in the distance. We slow our pace and I turn to him.

"And you two both have talents for being ignorant assholes."

He stops in his tracks, taken aback. My guilt immediately drowns me, "Ryder, I'm sorry, I'm just—"

He's walking briskly again, ahead of me, leading the way to the waiting women. "Come on," he says sharply. "Let's go make some soldiers."

THIRTY-THREE

"Positions!"

A handful of women are in front of me, thrusting, slashing and piercing their way into becoming stronger fighters. They are sweating viciously, every kick and punch executed with a triumphant flourish. They are happy to be here, to be learning, to finally be of use.

"Ava, how would you deflect a stab?" I turn behind me to see a grey-haired woman. She has been one of the most eager to learn, almost bouncing with excitement at every new move I add to their arsenal.

"Great question, Mary." I smile. She was the one who supported me when I first got here; who told everyone to trust me. Since then she's been invaluable in gaining the trust of others. She always invites Skyler and me to eat next to her and her son, Adam. "Like this." I show her the manoeuvre slowly, and then again at pace.

E . J .   E D E N

Only Carla, the young girl who has been hanging onto Ryder's shoulder since we arrived, looks unimpressed. She calls over from her position near me: "Shouldn't we be resting now?"

"Nope."

She shoots me a glare and continues to reluctantly wield her spear against her sparring partner. I am glad for the focus this provides – giving me time to shake off the encounter in the potato patch. After an hour, I'm fully focused. These women have real promise – more than I'd originally thought. But they need so much more work if they're going to stand against a Mute. Or a Guardian.

I started by asking the women to show me what they know. I watched as a handful demonstrated reasonably decent fighting technique. But all in all, the presentation of skills had been pretty underwhelming, which is worrying, despite how strong and fast they have the ability to be. These girls don't use their potential, and they are totally untrained.

I feel a disappointment in my estimation of Jayden; he's become slack with the training these women are receiving. I was glad that Ryder at least realized this and was able to convince his brother to let me train them. Jayden had agreed very reluctantly, arguing that there were so many other jobs that needed doing, he couldn't afford to be giving me time with them. But really, what could be more important than this: their ability to defend themselves?

Another jab, another punch. Or should I say: another weak attempt at a jab and a punch. I am increasingly irritated by Jayden's lack of vision with regards to his army. I shrug off the negative thoughts and mentally thank Ryder, who's been watching this whole time. He nods and disappears off for another strategy meeting.

After the initial display of their skills, I decide to move to basic weaponry. I teach them how to make weapons out of basic supplies. After some time, they have cobbled together bows and arrows, daggers and spears. The next few hours pass quickly with more training and sparring in the blistering heat. In just one session, their bodies have already learned how to pick up the pace and technique. I'm sure I can have them fighting fit and able to protect themselves by the time I leave for home.

By the time I leave.

Kai's wounded face pops into my mind, and I wonder if I'll ever get the chance to apologize before I do eventually leave for home. I quickly shake myself out of it and yell, "Alright, let's line up and ground yourself, work from your core, and we'll start again... Ready... FIGHT!"

The clearing explodes with movement: parrying, blocking and thrusting just like I've taught them. The older woman with grey-tinged hair – Mary – is shooting with her bow and arrow. She turns to me, beaming with her thumbs up at the shots she has just made. I smile back in approval: she's good.

Carla trudges closer to where I am watching from, in the shade of a nearby tree. "Dayna beat me twice now already," she says sullenly. "Can I go?

"No."

She grinds her teeth in frustration. "Look, I don't want to be here. Why make me stay? Let me go and not waste my time learning tricks from some Marked girl." Carla eyes me coldly. "A girl who thinks she's God's gift at fighting. We are naturally way stronger than the Guardians, like Jayden told us; they don't stand a chance against our strength and speed. I'll just use that." She smiles triumphantly at my stony silence, mistaking it for defeat. "I'm going back inside to look after the kids in the Carter," she adds defiantly.

I swallow my anger but as much as I try it bubbles to the surface. "You think you're safe here, don't you?"

"Of course I do."

"You never will be."

She takes a step back. "Is that a threat?" she hisses.

"No, it's a fact, Carla." I round on her, using all my restraint to keep my cool, but failing, yet again. "You've been lucky enough never to be caught out here and sent into Haven yourself. You think your strength and speed will allow you to fight against Guardians? Yeah, sure. Jayden may be right in telling you that's what they want from the prisoners back at Haven, but he hasn't told you about the details of their weaponry, the cars, the guns. They will rip you to shreds in an instant. Have you seen a gun, Carla? Have you seen what it can do? Do you even know what bullets are? One through your brain and you're dead. And even if you don't want to fight, if you want to let other people do it for you, then fine."

She starts to interject but something in my eyes must warn her not to.

"What happens," I say, "if they capture Resistance soldiers? If they torture them, and those soldiers cave? What if you are the only thing standing between them and that kid?" I point to the little boy, Max, who has been watching the sparring women with awe. He reminds me so much of Xander, of his curiosity and tenacity. My heart aches to see my brother.

Carla doesn't seem affected by my words one bit. She merely goes over to Max, picks him up, and struts inside.

That's when the screams start.

I whip my head around to see what the source of the noise is. I see all the girls that have been training standing dumbstruck, looks of horror etched over all of their faces.

From the edge of the tree line near to where we have been working there emerges a man carrying a young boy, no more than sixteen, with blood soaked over his entire body. I recognize them both from the first day I arrived. The boy's arm is gone. "No!" I hear a scream. It's Mary. A sickening realization dawns upon me: the boy is Adam, her son.

I burst into action, crossing the distance within seconds. Ryder is way behind me but with my weakened adapts, we arrive simultaneously.

He takes control of the situation immediately. Mary is cradling Adam, she beat us both to him.

"What happened?" Ryder demands.

"Mutes," the man replies.

My blood turns cold.

"Two of them. We were out hunting. We were outnumbered. Tyler, he didn't make it. Leah, she was with us. We lost her. I told her to run so she did."

The older man grunts in pain. He has scars running down his arms and one on his cheek, but otherwise he looks alright. The boy, on the other hand, has passed out from blood loss. I gingerly inspect the boy's arm, assessing the damage. The limb has been ripped clean off.

"Ava, get him to the infirmary. Now," Ryder orders. Something stops me momentarily. There is something about this man's demeanour – something isn't right.

"How long ago?" I ask.

The man takes a gulp of air and looks down. He doesn't answer me.

"How long?" I press.

"Not five minutes ago."

Ryder's and my eyes widen at the same time.

"You left a blood trail with Mutes on your tail five minutes away from here?" Ryder looks sick to the stomach.

I turn on my heel and yell to everyone in the clearing. The clearing is about a three-minute run from camp. There's no assurance we'll make it. "Get inside, get back to the Observatory!" I yell. "NOW!"

There's nothing we can do to stop it.

They are coming.

THIRTY-FOUR

A low growl rips through the clearing. I whirl to see five bright red, cat-like eyes lined horizontally on a Mute's huge oval skull. Its hackles are up, its fur is ruffled and it's scanning for the nearest piece of prey it can see.

Oh.

That would be me, then.

It launches towards me, crossing the distance between us almost instantly, claws and teeth scratching at me, trying to grab hold. I roll to the side, recovering quickly, grabbing my knife from where it sits on the strap on my thigh.

"Come on then!" I yell.

The Mute launches itself at me in attack, and again I roll, removing myself from claws much too close for my liking. I stab at its gut. No luck. I feel a rush of air and see arrows sailing toward the Mute. A few hit home on its feline shoulders but it seems to barely register it. My strength isn't where it usually is, and I know it's just a matter of time before it has me cornered. But I need to give the others time to run.

"No! Stay back!" I yell to the women attempting to aid me. If they aggravate it, it will leave me and go for them. I draw back and attempt another few stabs, feigning and ducking to confuse it. But I am now too much effort.

It has seen its next prey.

One of Mary's arrows hits true, right into one of the five eyes. The Mute howls in agony. "That's for my son, you bastard!" she screams wildly. It runs for her. She fires as quickly as she can, arrow after arrow, but the bow is all she has, and even her near-perfect shots barely seem to affect this Mute. They aren't close enough to its heart. It's a strong one. With a rip and a scream, it bites into her flesh.

Her horrified look, how she watches this thing take a bite out of her so easily, so without feeling, so driven only by raw hunger, will be with me until the day I die. "NO!" I scream, but it is drowned by Mary's scream of agony: a long, low thing coming up from her gut and echoing from her mouth. The other women around her panic and scatter. Her knees buckle. I am too far away, but I try to run to her, frustrated by my still-slowed reactions, my horrible, torturously slow feet.

Ryder is there in seconds, way before me, but he's already too late. Instantly he is on top of the Mute, stabbing at his eyes, wrestling it and riding it and fighting it all at once. He holds onto its head to avoid the jaws snapping at him. He throws one arm up in the air, catching a spear that Jayden has sent from across the clearing. The spear strikes home in the Mute's skull with deadly precision. The beast collapses under his weight, giving a final few kicks with its paws before becoming still.

I run to Mary, lifting her into my arms. From the look of her wounds around her neck and shoulder, the Mute has hit a vital artery. Blood gushes everywhere making my own body sticky and red. She'd tried to help me. To save my life. She tries to gurgle a few words, but blood is the only thing that surfaces. "It's ok," I say. "Adam is safe. Thanks to you, he is safe. He's going to be fine." I rock her quietly until she is still, her glassy eyes never seeing the grieving group who now surround her.

THIRTY-FIVE

I sit next to Skyler at dinner. I'm staring outside towards where Mary took her final breaths, pushing the food around my plate. "You need to eat, Ava." Skyler eyes me worriedly. "Please eat."

Everyone is still in shock and not much has been said after the burial. Most eat in silence, staring off at some unknown presence in the distance. Jayden walks in and all eyes fix themselves on him. "Ava," he calls quietly and gestures to the next room. I stand, and Skyler follows suit until Jayden commands, "Just Ava please."

Skyler throws me a sideways glance but sits back down next to Lucy, who is nibbling half-heartedly at some game, tears welling in her eyes. "Give me a yell if you need anything."

I walk slowly and ignore the glares that are emulating from all sides as I cross the room. Within the first few days I've been here, they've been attacked and lost a soldier, apparently something that hasn't happened in ten months. I can sense their fear, their distrust. I know that none of this has inspired confidence in my presence.

I step into a room that looks like some sort of office, with papers and plans sprawled over every possible surface. I see the older man named Tex, one of the Resistance's older soldiers, and Ryder standing at the back of the room, deep in an intense conversation. On the other side of the room Kai stands awkwardly, his hands in his pockets, his weight constantly shifting as though he doesn't know what to do with himself. He turns as I walk into the room, his expression growing even more sombre, eyebrows furrowed, the colour leaving his face at a rapid rate.

"What's up?" I ask, trying to sound lighter than I feel – than anyone feels. I know suspicion is growing by the second. And now mine is, too. Something feels off.

"Leah's gone missing," Jayden says.

I halt in my tracks. "What? Is she ok? What happened?"

"She was with the hunting party that took on the Mute. And Luke, the man that carried Adam in today. He said she went missing before that."

"Oh, well that's a relief," I say. "At least, she wasn't hurt or attacked by the Mute, right? She'll still be out there."

"That's what I said," Ryder interjects. "Until this one..." he gestures towards Kai with a jerk of his head, "...came to Jayden with a bit of information."

"Information?" I ask. What information did Kai have on Leah?

Kai turns towards me, his eyes deep caverns of worry. "Ava, you've gotta listen to me. I was trying to protect—"

"Oh shut up," Tex grunts. "You've compromised us all."

I turn to him, not letting him escape my eyes. "Kai. What have you done?"

He gulps. "You know that conversation you overheard Leah and me having when I was on watch, the first night after we escaped?"

I think back to the forest, my interruption of their conversation, his discomfort. I remember him asking me if I'd heard everything that was said. My pulse picks up. "Yeah, I do."

"Well, she wanted us to run away together, like I told you that night. Just the two of us. She figured between Mutes and Chosen we wouldn't stand much of a chance surviving alone, so she wanted to strike a deal with the Doctor and the other Chosen back in Haven. She knows the Doctor wants you, above everyone else, for whatever he's got planned." He's speaking fast now, and it's all pouring out while my mind tries to keep up. "She would never give up the Resistance. She didn't want innocent people to die. But she wanted you. She wanted to exchange you for the guarantee of our safety."

"She—what? No... No, you're wrong. We talked – she... She wouldn't do that. I didn't hear her say that." My lip begins to tremble. I bite down on my tongue to stop it. I can taste the sharp tang of blood.

"Apparently this idiot over here convinced her not to, but now he's scared that because she's gone missing – that's what she's gone to do, which is why it has been brought to our attention. Nice of you to drop that little bomb on us, mate," Ryder says.

I search Kai's eyes, his face, every part of him, willing it not to be true. He looks back in dismay. "We don't know that's what she's done. She could be lost out there! She could still be with us, still be loyal to us. She wouldn't have done it. I know it was just words. She knows how important you are to me, Ava. I am *so* sorry." Tears stream down his cheeks, he goes to grab my hands but I snatch them away from him, stepping back toward Ryder. His head hangs low.

"Unlikely story," Tex says. "A rat is a rat and you're just as bad. Trying to save her from our judgement, trying to protect a coward, and now you've compromised our position."

"She wouldn't give up all of the Resistance's lives! I swear. She knew Ava wasn't going to be harmed – the Doctor just wants her for something else. He's kept her safe all that time, and he let her go without shooting her that day at the cliff."

Kai's attempt at an explanation falls on deaf ears. No one is listening. But he continues just the same, determined to help his friend. "And that's why he wanted to exchange Skyler for Ava, don't you see? He's only after Ava. You're safe here. I swear your location won't be compromised. Leah wouldn't betray the Resistance."

After all this time I thought Kai had been there for me, and now here he was defending the girl who had just betrayed me. If she compromises my position for her guaranteed safety, then she could destroy the Resistance. If they find me, they find the Resistance and we're done. Everyone in here is dead. It's unlikely that there are enough humans left out in the wild to learn of the Chosen from another Resistance and save all of us. It'd be over. I gasp in and out.

"How can we be sure of that?" Jayden shouts. "I won't let my people be in danger for your guess work!" Jayden launches straight into a plan of attack, diligent as always, his face and gestures fierce. "We need to move. Ryder, these people aren't ready to attack Haven, not after today. It took us years to find a place as protected and fortified as this, and if we lose more soldiers to Mutes out there ... we'll never get another shot. What do we do?"

Ryder's response comes but I can't hear it. I think back to the conversation Leah and I had on top of the Carter. My skin prickles as I click the puzzle pieces into place. "She knows," I mutter.

"What was that?"

"She knows. I—I told her where my family are hiding out. Where our cave is. Two nights ago, on the top of the Observatory. She wouldn't betray the Resistance, but she'd betray *me*. And that's what she's going to do. She's going back to tell White Suit where my family is, so he has leverage over me. So I'll find *him*. He won't even have to try to search for me. If … if he's got my family, if she tells him where they are, he'll know I'll go back to Haven for them."

The room is still. I break the silence by pushing past Kai, giving him one last look of disgust before I leave. "Ave—" He reaches for me.

"DON'T touch me." I send daggers in my stare and he takes a few steps back. I burst out of the room, not noticing the sea of faces looking at me. Leah needs to get back to Haven so she can tell White Suit where they are. If she left this afternoon, she's already be halfway back there. And once she tells him and they use those trucks …

Time is running out.

I only have one option; to get them safe and hidden before White Suit beats me there.

It's time to go home.

THIRTY-SIX

I don't acknowledge Ryder when he steps into the room, although I sense he's close behind me. It's only been five short minutes since I've left Kai and the others.

"Jayden thinks it's too dangerous. He's ordered you not to go. It's my job to make sure those orders are obeyed."

I laugh mirthlessly. "You honestly think I am going to listen to you?"

I am standing in the women's dorm room collecting anything I can find that may be of use to me. My backpack lies on the bed in front of me, already stuffed full.

Kai. He'd protected Leah over me. My heart feels like it might shatter and explode. Shaking myself, I shove those feelings deep down: those can't be priorities. I can do this. I can be cold-blooded. I guess Mum was always right: trust can kill as easily as a blade.

I shove the backpack onto my shoulders. Three handguns, one rifle, some rope and three knives are strapped into various hidden places on my body. I've quickly changed into hunting gear that the Resistance acquired – they call it camouflage. It covers most areas of my body, but I have also used a black belt to cinch in my waist. My usually wild hair is now pulled back into a severe bun. As I swing myself around to prepare to leave, I see Ryder now, there in the doorway. He has been examining me from behind. I was blocking him out, but his intensity is hard to escape now. His eyes are on my body; they move up it slowly, finally – reluctantly – arriving at my face. I pause at the heat in his eyes.

Snap out of it. Xander is in Danger.

My mind echoes with that fact and immediately I am brought back to the task at hand. "Move," I say firmly.

But he doesn't. Instead, he turns and shuts the door, locking it behind him, and putting the key he's just produced back into his pocket.

"What the hell are you doing?" I can tell he is trying not to squirm.

"Jayden's orders. You're not to go anywhere other than this dorm room, at least until we figure out our plan of attack. You don't know Leah has given away the location of your family. You're just guessing."

I lunge for his pocket. He pushes me back firmly. I leap at him again.

I flail around, punching, kicking, scratching – anything I can do to stop him from overpowering me, but he weighs at least a third more than me. I am stuck in a bear hug he has used to keep me contained and immobile.

Damn damn damn damn. I need to get to them before it's too late.

My struggling begins to slow and then I stop struggling altogether. Our eyes meet. He relaxes his body but his face is still strained, his eyes apprehensively bearing into my own. "I'm just following orders. It's what any good soldier would do."

"Ok," I say.

"I want to keep you safe."

"Ok."

"Because I think I'm in love with you."

I pause.

"Ok..."

His admission is so simple, so soft, so honest. Everything I have been holding in, every emotion I have experienced over the past few days begins to bubble up to the surface, overwhelming me.

My face is suddenly wet. I cry for all the people still stuck in Haven, being tortured and hurt every day. I cry because I haven't helped them. I cry for the family I don't know if I'll ever see again. I cry for my mother and the memory of her smile and her broken body in my arms and her unseeing eyes, eyes just like Mary's.

And Ryder holds me there. He holds me as I break and the words he has just said sink in and put me back together, piece by piece.

Slowly, I stop crying.

Ryder pulls me down onto the bed, and I'm now seated next to him. He watches me. I am on fire under his gaze, ashamed of what has just passed between us: it feels too intimate to be here like this with him. Too vulnerable.

He breathes out sigh, before turning back to me. "The only girl I've said, 'I love you' to, and she starts crying. Not quite the way I saw that panning out." I grin back, hiccupping at the same time. "I know you want to go," he says, focused, "but we've got to think of the greater good, right? All those people still stuck there – the Marked – they're relying on us."

I nod, knowing that everything that he has ever done, everything that has seemed cruel or cold or hard, he's done because he thought it was what needed to be done. He's done it because it was the right thing to do. He's trying to help hundreds of people. I lift my eyes to his, those sure and steady amber eyes. I put my hand on his cheek, tracing his jaw with my thumb gently.

Our kiss is tentative, wary. We are slightly awkward and aware of each other, as if we both know this isn't really the answer that he wanted from his admission of love, but he responds all the same. Our bodies seem to know what the other needs. His tongue gently brushes my own. I grab his hair to encourage him to continue. Our hands begin to roam, tracing each other's bodies, setting fire to the nerves beneath our skin.

His eyes are closed, and he is trying to kiss away my pain but he is failing.

Mine are open as I reach for the gun he is carrying on his belt behind him.

As I click the safety off and aim at his head, he freezes mid-kiss, breaking away from me.

His eyes scorch my own, questioning me, testing me. "You wouldn't," he says.

"Try me," I reply, my eyes narrowing.

I am obviously convincing.

He gulps and I see sweat break out on his forehead at the threat. Without taking my eyes off of him I reach for the rope in the bag. "Tie your feet up and sit down on the bed." He concedes, and the hurt on his face almost murders me right there.

"Your brother is wrong to try to control me. I'm not giving up the people I love for his cause." I reach for the key in his pocket, my lips brushing a gentle kiss on his neck as I do it.

He shakes his head and grimaces, "You really are something else."

My reply is a brisk kiss on his lips before I walk out of the dorm, locking the door behind me.

I almost crash into Skyler as I turn the corner, each of us sprinting up the hallway to a different destination. "I just heard. They told me they locked you away. I agreed it was the right thing to do just so they'd let me go. I was coming to rescue you."

"Didn't need help this time, but thanks," I grin. Skyler will always stand with me, and we both know it. But it is reassuring all the same to know she is here, ready to fight with me. As we sneak a look around the corner to the main hall, I balk.

Most of the Resistance are there, and Jayden is addressing them from the podium. We both throw our hoods up, hiding our faces, and make casually for the door. My theory is when in doubt, act like you own the place: if no one recognizes us then we can stroll out of here with no questions asked. That's the theory anyway. Time to test it.

"...and of course we are not going to take this matter lightly. We have search parties being sent out. We are confident we can capture Leah before she gets to Haven and reveals our position. She will answer to her crimes of betrayal by pain of death. That's all the information I can release right now. Go back to your posts."

The room erupts with activity as Jayden steps down from his wooden podium. He heads straight to a map, pointing out different areas for people to cover in the search for Leah. The room is such a flurry of activity no one can see past a few feet of themselves. The last thing on anyone's mind are the hooded figures on the outskirts of the hall, slowly making their way to the door.

"How are we going to get out of here?" Skyler mutters as we squeeze past a group of people talking animatedly about which quadrant they have been assigned.

"Just walk slowly and act casual," I barely breathe out loud enough for her to hear. We have almost made it out when a voice stops us in our tracks.

"What are you doing?"

I roll my eyes as I see who's at the door, watching all the action from afar. Of course he would stay out of everyone's way; this is all his fault. My fury at Kai had been like an explosion before, but now it is numbed under the importance of my task; I'll deal with it later.

"We're leaving. And don't try to stop us." I point the gun at his stomach, the weapon hidden from the others by my jacket. Kai's eyes are begging me to see reason. I see keys for one of the few trucks the Resistance has in its possession hanging on Kai's weapons belt. "Give me those."

"Ava, don't." I hear true panic in his voice.

"Now," I spit.

Kai hands them to me reluctantly.

"And by the way," I say as I breeze past him – I want to make him hurt as much as he hurt me. I know it's wrong and it's cruel and it's harsh but it escapes my mouth anyway, hanging in the air between us, "We're done. You're no longer my friend. You are no longer *anything* to me."

His face crumples, eyes changing from disbelief to anger to heartbreak all in one instant and we stay there, locked in that moment, almost too afraid to move. I turn on my heel and an acid bubbles up inside me, attacking every cell. My eyes sting from it.

"That was pretty cruel," Skyler says.

Yes, it was, I'll admit. But he'd hurt me too. He was supposed to be my friend. He'd chosen Leah over my safety. He might have given my family a death sentence.

I turn the keys around in my hand uncomfortably as we run for the truck. Our feet pounding on the pavement is the only sound in the still night.

We jump into the truck. I turn the key and don't look back at the boy standing there, alone, watching me leave.

THIRTY-SEVEN

The note is hidden where he knows I'll find it.

Ava,

I don't know what's happened to you or where you are, but I know you'll be trying to get back to us.

Some strange things started to happen a few weeks after you and Skyler left. From up here, I saw trucks and men dressed in black with huge rifles and tanks – seemed like they were looking for something, or someone.

The men looked dangerous.

I knew it'd only be a matter of time before they started looking up, above their usual line of sight – that they'd start to search everywhere possible. They never strayed more than a few kilometres from here. They were looking for something ... my feeling is that it was you.

I knew it wasn't safe to stay, so Xander and I had to leave. My injury will hold us up a little, but I know that something's not right here.

I wish I knew a safe place to go and say I'll meet you there – but it's too dangerous to write down anyway.

I hope you understand that leaving here without you was the hardest decision of my life, but those people – they felt wrong.

Xander asks after you every day. He has nightmares when you aren't here with him. I have faith you will find us one day.

Xander and I love you very much,

Dad

I am frozen as I read. Again and again I stare at the letters until they no longer make sense. I stare around me at the rubble that had once been my home. The cave has been ransacked. There was the pile of books I had found in Wellington. I had picked up my favorite book, *Call It Courage*, and the note had slipped out.

Skyler stands by watching me read and re-read before finally deciding to snatch the paper off me, willing her brain to understand the words that she can't decipher. Mum insisted on teaching me how to read when I was younger. I can't read much but its been enough to get me by. Skyler's past hadn't afforded her such luxuries. I'd had to teach her what I could over the past few years. She had caught on fast, but even so, reading takes time – not something we have a lot of.

"What does it say?" Skyler asks impatiently.

"They left. Guardians had been hanging around and Dad got scared. I don't know where they are."

Skyler sits quickly, her legs giving out on her. Her head swivels up to mine every now and then, each time her expression alters slightly: disbelief, grief, anger.

Tears sting at my vision, blinding me. My body feels hot and cold at the same time. Bile pushes up my throat, willing itself out of my body. I force it back down.

"Ok. So we scour the perimeter. We go back to Haven and watch for signs that they're there. If they are, we break them out. If they aren't, we keep looking." Skyler says. I nod mutely at her strategy. I understand that this is how she has learnt to cope. From what she'd told me about her past, it would be a lot to bear. She can be calculating – but it's essential for us to survive. To move at the pace that we need to.

I propel myself into action, scouting the smashed objects strewn over the floor, seeing what we can use to our advantage. Our truck had run out of petrol, so we'd be heading out again on foot. The truck would have to be abandoned to the mercy of the wild.

"Dad and Xander are still out there, alive – I know it," I say.

"It's going to be ok," she says, I can't help feeling like she's trying to convince herself, "We'll find them."

We scramble through the contents of what is left of our cave, finding nothing of use. Dad and Xander have taken everything that would be useful for them to survive: all my bows, my spear. I am glad they have those items; it gives me a strange sense of calm to know they have something of mine protecting them.

I see Xander's old favourite book about a hungry caterpillar sitting in the dust of the cave floor, its pages tattered and worn. He had been so excited the day I'd given it to him. He must have been six at the time. He'd asked me to read it to him about ten times that night. It had driven me slightly crazy at the time; why didn't he understand that I had routes to plan for our next hunt, and game to skin and cook? That we needed to find other places to raid where there would be no chance of running into other human groups or Mutes? My mind had been far away and I'd raced through the pages, growing slightly more irritated each time he'd asked me to repeat the story.

Now, I pick the book up, fold the loose pages of my father's note into my pocket and tuck the book into a backpack I'd found. One day I'll return it to him. Even if he is eight and won't read it anymore.

I pause at the ridge of the cave. I think back to the last time I left this place; how much simpler everything was back then. "I'll be back," I promise the cave. But even I can hear the doubt in my voice, the slight quiver that indicates otherwise. It does not fill me with confidence; it only recalls the memory of my mother. *"I'm right behind you,"* she had said.

I see Skyler far below. I start to scale down the cliff, my mind wandering back to memories of Mum.

We don't stand a chance. The attack is swift.

Skyler screams for me to run at the bottom of the cliff as a bullet rips into her arm. A bullet or something else? I don't get the chance to find out.

I am shot, too. I can't tell where they are coming from. They're not bullets: they stick out of me, like a needle. I try to rip them out of my skin but it's too late.

A blue ink is spreading on my body, highlighting the veins around the wound. I run towards where Skyler has fallen.

"Skyler? SKYLER! Talk to me. C'mon, Skyler, wake up. Wake up." I shake and roll her. There's no response, but I can see the rise and fall of her chest. It's as if she's in a deep sleep. My brain begins to feel slow and hazy. My legs give in and I fall next to her, clawing on the rocks to get away from whoever has attacked us.

Black spots blur my vision before overtaking it completely. My limbs become paralyzed and I can no longer move.

My last thought is of Dad.

THIRTY-EIGHT

As if jolted from a bad dream, I regain consciousness quickly and suddenly. Opening my eyes doesn't do me much good. It's pitch black. The trucks a few hundred metres away from me indicate that there are humans around, but none are present. I feel a sting at my wrists and look toward the pain.

I am bound.

Metal cables have rendered my feet and hands useless. I glance around and see the person I am looking for: Skyler. She is lying next to me, unconscious, but breathing. I huff a sigh of relief.

"*Skyler*," I hiss, pushing my feet toward her and shoving her own in an attempt to rouse her. I see little bruises painting the veins around the spots where she was hit with whatever it was that shot us. I look at my own body: the same. Black veins surround angry red marks, several all over my body. Whatever those things were, they've left evidence on both of us.

I pull at the wires that tie me together. Nothing. They don't budge one bit. These wires are normally something I could break any day of the week. A black fog of fear encloses around me. I must be back to depleted strength. The wires burn my skin as I struggle further. I almost burst into tears as I realize my supernatural strength will not return to me on command.

We must have been drugged. *Again.*

"That's really not going to help." It's a voice I don't recognize.

I turn to count seven men and four women as they emerge from the bushes, all in what looks like Guardian uniforms, but they're slightly altered. The Chosen insignia on their sleeves is there for all to see, but it's a different colour to what they wear in Haven: a forest green as opposed to the original black.

They all hold guns trained at my face. No one moves an inch.

I can tell which one has addressed me as her eyes never stray from their target: me. A foot shorter than the others, she stands with a slightly odd stance, pushing her chest up further than it wants to go. With such a straight posture it looks as if she may topple over any second. "The darts we hit you with hinder your ability, sadly," she says, not looking sad at all.

"Good, so it'll be a fair fight then," I reply. "I hate winning too quickly."

A bark of a laugh. "Now, I could be wrong, but I have a feeling I'm not: you're the famous Ava the Doctor is looking for."

I say nothing but wiggle up to a kneeling position as she draws closer.

"Ah, so I'm guessing this is Skyler then." Her boot presses Skyler's cheek further into the ground, leaving angry marks.

"Don't touch her," I spit.

She rounds on me and growls, "Or what?"

I decide to hold my tongue. In the silence simmering between this stranger and me, Skyler wakes groggily, alarm igniting her face when she sees the situation at hand.

"Surely as a *Marked* you should know when to pay respect to your superiors," the woman proudly announces, puffing her chest out even further. "We are Hunters, a division of Guardians that finds outsiders that have been unclaimed. We bring them into Haven so they can ... *stay* with the Doctor and his Chosen ones." She grins.

"You mean you take them back for slaughter. And testing. So you can figure out how to become more like us. Because you never survived the Cull – you just avoided it."

The Guardians' faces fall into worry and confusion.

"Tell me, Ash," I sneer her name and her knuckles flex as I do. "How does it feel to be the inferior one out of the two of us? With my strength, when it comes back, I could kill you in a few seconds flat. Pity you guys will never be able to figure out how the scum Marked work, huh? People like Skyler, and I."

Her fist connects with my face with a loud *thwack*. I don't give her the satisfaction of crying out in pain. I spit the blood out, my stare never leaving her eyes. "Not so tough now, are you?" she cackles. The ripple of laughter echoes through the forest and I idly wonder if a Mute might just hear, approach silently, and then kill her for me. A brief fantasy. But then I think about how it would kill us too so I shake the thought right out of my mind.

"What does the Doctor want with Ava?" Skyler asks boldly.

Ash shrugs and struts back towards her group of Hunters. "How should I know? I just bring people in." She winks to demonstrate to us she knows otherwise, savouring the thrill of knowing whatever awful things White Suit wants to do with me.

"So that's where we're going?" Skyler's face falls. "Back to Haven?" We look towards each other in panic.

"You should feel lucky. If it were up to me, I would have killed you as soon as we found you," Ash says casually, inspecting the dirt under her fingernails. "But ... Doctor's orders." She turns to the other Guardians. "However, we do have one more little problem that needs to be dealt with before we get that far. So, you're staying here. Cole, Delia, you're on first watch. Just get those Marked scum outta my sight."

THIRTY-NINE

"What do you think they were talking about, getting rid of a problem?" Skyler asks. "You don't think they have your family, do you?" Her voice increases in pitch.

"No," I reply firmly. "They would be at this camp with us if they were. And Ash would have used that to taunt me if the Hunters had found and captured them."

I'm fairly certain my family are safe. I have a good feeling. It's pretty weird, but I can usually sense when Xander is in trouble. My tummy feels off and I feel ill, or things just ... don't fit into place.

"Do you think the Resistance will come and save us?" she asks hopefully.

My heart shrinks a little in my chest. "No," I reply. "I think I made it pretty clear to them that I don't want their help anymore." I think of Ryder tied up in the dorm room and roll my eyes at the irony of the bonds now stopping my own hands from moving.

"What do you think White Suit wants from you?"

"I don't *know* Skyler. I'm trying to think of a way out of this, so just please stop talking."

"Sor-ry." She sing-songs her apology, rolling her eyes.

No solutions for escaping come to me, despite the silence.

We sit there for hours attempting to wriggle subtly to loosen our bonds whenever we can get the chance – when that idiot of a Guardian isn't either watching us or mocking us from afar.

A few hours of quiet struggling later, I hear a command that comes in from a little black box attached to our guard's belt, just a few metres away. There is sound coming from it. Ryder had shown me his when I was in Haven and explained what it does. Some kind of immediate communication device, I think he called it a *radio*. I didn't think much of it at the time, and I had forgotten about those types of technology – but now I lean in to listen. I hear a few words – and a man's voice.

"Carter to Hunter base. Carter to Hunter base. Red Game is ready to be executed. We will not tell the Doctor any locations until we have all of them captured or killed. If we finish the job before they even know about the problem, we will be rewarded. Giving them the information won't mean as much to them. We need to do it ourselves. We move at dawn. Over." The Guard smiles at the new information that has just been passed through the device.

The rough voice sounds familiar, but through the crackle, it could be anyone.

Then another voice, a female, answers back through the channel. I'm pretty sure it's Ash. "Hunter Base to Carter. Copy that. After Red Game we will continue with a ground attack. Over."

The other voice comes back: "See you shortly. Over." There is a smile in the man's voice.

Things click into place all too quickly. "Carter as in Carter Observatory?" I explode at the Guardian on watch.

He turns around grinning idiotically. His eyes shine with glee. "Yep," he says. "People say the Hunter Guardians are stupid and not good enough to be real Guardians, but *we* found the Resistance base and *we're* gonna blow it up. *Boom.* We'll all be rewarded when we present you and the rest of the Resistance to the Doctor. We might even become Chosen ourselves." His chest puffs with pride. "And we've even got a man on the inside now, helping us kill all of you scum. Your own people are turning against you. We're gonna blow it to smithereens." He walks over to Skyler and grabs her face in his hands. She takes a bite at his fingers but he extracts them in time and slaps her instead. "Stupid Marked bitch..."

At that exact moment an arrow flies from a far tree into his jugular. Blood spurts all over Skyler's face. She yells in shock as he falls to the ground and her head snaps to me in panic.

What the hell just happened?

I don't wait for an answer. This is our chance. Skyler is frozen on the floor. "Try to get the knife on his belt," I command. She begins to struggle, jutting her feet out towards the fallen body.

The other Guardians run towards me, yelling in fury for their fallen comrade. As if I'm not the one tied up right now. More arrows descend from above, raining down on the Hunters. The Hunters jump and dodge in panic, shooting their guns in the air, unable to see where the arrows are coming from. Ash pulls the curtain of her tent up, her facing grimacing in horror as a further two men are shot to the ground before her.

Most of the men start running toward the trucks. Sensible enough for them. Unfortunately, Skyler and I are not able to escape quite so easily, being tied up and all.

"Hey!" I shout to them in desperation. But no one hears me as they jump into their trucks, and speed away. Ash is yelling at them to get back to their posts and then seems to see sense, jumping into a truck of her own. We are all but forgotten as they drive off without us.

I reach for the fallen Guardian with my hands still tied together. I manage to awkwardly shift them in the ropes and pry the arrow out of his neck, blood pumping onto the grass below us, making a sticky pool around us. I begin to ravage the ties with as much force as I possibly can, splitting it little by little, but I know it's not enough. The attackers will get here any minute now and then we'll be …

And that's when I see her. About fifty metres away from me, she scales down the tree and turns to us triumphantly, placing a bow on her back.

Leah.

FORTY

Leah unbinds me, slicing the knife through my restraints in one swoop.

Immediately I launch myself at her, arms outstretched like a wildcat. She is knocked onto her back, too shocked to respond to my sudden outburst. I don't think this is the welcome she expects from me. Good, I can attack her while she's down. All of my fury pours out of me.

"Stop!" Skyler yells, as I go to punch Leah in the face. Pain shatters through my knuckles and my hand feels like broken glass.

What the—

And then I remember the darts that had just been shot at me, weakening me, probably reverting me back to the strength of a Marked. Her eyes flash with the realization, and with one hand she clasps my neck and shoves me to the side. Her hold on me is unbreakable; any harder and she could snap my neck. She rolls me over until I am the one pinned down.

"What was that for?!" she yells. "I just saved your ass!"

"Only because you want to sell me out. And my *family*. How dare you!"

Leah's eyes cloud with confusion and her hold relaxes a little. Pins and needles tingle where her hand had been. I use the opportunity to shove her off me and get to a position where I can attack: standing, feet apart, guard up and ready to go. Not like it's going to be of any use against her, but still worth a shot – and better than getting beaten with your hands restrained.

"What are you talking about?"

"You know what I'm talking about, Leah!"

"No, really. I don't."

My resolve falters for a moment as I scan her confused face. "You left when Adam got attacked by those Mutes," I say. "He was your opportunity out. You went back to White Suit to tell him where my family was, so he can use them for whatever sick game he's playing with me in exchange for your safety. You asked Kai to come with you before, but he wouldn't. So, you left yourself. You betrayed me." She flinches at Kai's name, shaking her head, but I continue with the story I have compiled together. "You sold us out. That's what Kai told us you planned to do, and that you had tried to get him to help you as soon as we left Haven. As soon as *we* got you out."

"No, that's not what happened, Ava. Listen to me." Her tone is urgent, "I got split up from the others when the Mute attacked, and I had no choice but to run and hide." She shudders a little and carries on. "I just kept running, I didn't think about the fact that Guardians were still out there looking for us. I got captured by the Hunters when I was out in the wild. They took me, and they were getting ready to take me back to permanent testing." She waits for my response.

I say nothing. She grinds her teeth a little in the silence that follows.

"I was stuck *here*. I never sold you or your family out, I swear. After Micah rescued me, I stayed with his group. That night with Kai – I was stupid. I was terrified. I said some things I didn't mean – that I'd never follow through on. Ever. I was a coward." Her perfect face grimaces.

Skyler is still tied up and has been watching us with her mouth gaping a little. Her head snaps back and forth to each of us in confusion. "So you're saying you never betrayed us? That you've been a captive of the Hunter Guardians all this time?" she asks.

"Until Micah saved me, yes."

"Wait, hold up. Who's Micah?" At that exact moment I hear a thud and turn to see a boy, who looks a little younger than me, maybe sixteen. The branches rustling above us tell me where he'd just come from.

"That would be me." His eyes gleam with mischief as stalks out from under the tree and stands next to Leah. He wears camouflage pants and a dark jersey with a hood, which he still has up. Six more young boys emerge from the trees, bows and arrows all in hand. The youngest is probably about twelve. I smile smugly at the fact that these seven teens have just scared off trained soldiers of Haven single-handedly. Leah squeezes Micah's arm and it doesn't take a genius to see the adoration on his face. My eyes arch up in a question and she smiles back knowingly.

"You're a good shot, Micah. All of you are. Thank you for saving our lives," I say.

Micah nods his head once in acknowledgement but expands no more on the tale that Leah has been telling us.

Skyler pipes up, "Right, so now we've all figured out we're on the same team can someone untie me please?"

We all chuckle and the tension breaks. Micah walks over to Skyler and begins the task of freeing her from the wires that bind her. As I turn to Leah, the acid in my stomach rises again and my mind snaps back into focus. Everyone at the Carter – they are all in danger.

"Leah, listen to me. The Resistance, they're in trouble. A Hunter Guardian had a radio – and I overheard something. There's someone back at the Observatory, someone who has betrayed the Resistance. He was talking about the *Red Game*. The Hunter said they know where the Carter is, and they are going to blow it up and attack anyone that survives. They are going to destroy the Resistance."

Leah's eyes widen in horror. "Micah, what's the quickest way to the Observatory from here?" she asks.

"If we run fast we could make it in an hour, maybe two." He replies.

"My friends back at the Carter – they're in trouble, Micah. Can you help us?"

"Of course."

I can see that there is be no other answer for Micah. He's ready and willing to fight. The other boys behind him all nod solemnly. I wonder where their parents are for a moment and then stop myself from asking – there's no time for that right now.

"Wait." Skyler says just before we take off. "Ava and I were hit by weakening darts – like the injections in Haven."

Damn. She's right. We wouldn't be able to keep up with them. We might not make it in time.

Leah thinks for a moment before an answer comes. She bends down, gesturing to me to ride on her back whilst she runs. "Hop on."

"We'll slow you down," I say. "You guys should just go, I'll figure out a way to get us there."

"I know you will, but if it comes to hand-to-hand combat, we need you. Even when you're weak, you're a better fighter than most soldiers back at the Carter."

Her answers are short and clipped. I see a strength and certainty in her that impresses me. She seems like a different girl to the quivering thing in the permanent-testing room. I nod in agreement and jump onto her back. Micah scoops Skyler up into his arms, carrying her like the way I used to carry Xander when he was a baby. She blushes every shade of pink possible.

But there is no time for her mortification: they set off at a blistering pace, and Leah and I follow.

FORTY-ONE

Eyes and mouths freeze as we step into the hall of the Observatory.

Conversations fall away until a painful silence is all that surrounds us. Everyone is in the main hall, gathered around what looks like a map. The aroma of petrol and cooked meat fills the air with a sharp tang.

We pause at the door, Skyler next to me; Leah and Micah and the rest of his group trailing a few steps behind. I look to Leah and nod my head in encouragement. She pastes on a convincing smile and turns it towards all of the Resistance members, staring at her with a mix of fury and confusion; they all still think she'd betrayed us, like I did. I'm sure they are wondering why she would show her face again and not expect to be locked up, or worse.

This time, I don't feel nervous to speak, but my body still tightens up under the hot gaze of the room. I see Ryder before he sees me; his jaw is locked and tight as he scans the map. He lifts his head and his eyes meet mine. I suddenly feel warm. He arches an eyebrow, fighting back a grin of excitement, obviously thinking back to our last encounter.

Kai is thin-lipped at the sight of both Leah and me. He seems slightly removed from the others, and almost uninterested in the action that is sure to unfold at our reappearance. Jayden is next to Ryder, the broad planes of his chest hunched over the map. As he looks at us, his jaw begins to tense and the worry in his eyes turns to fury. His voice is quiet and even but the aggression in his tone is unmistakable.

"Ava, Skyler, nice of you to join us. Funny you drop in after I specifically ordered you not to leave under any circumstances." The smile he shares is for show.

My gaze fights itself away from the group and I focus on the one I need to convince. "We're in trouble," I state simply, directly to him.

"I know we are. Do you not see the traitor behind you? You girls buddies now? It is quite possible and extremely probable that she has told the Doctor and his Chosen where we are." Jayden seems all too quick to make decisions. "Ryder, take them all. Lock them in a holding cell."

"Wait!" The lonely echo of my voice rings through the hall. "She never betrayed us. Leah saved us from Hunter Guardians and they are on their way here, right now."

The room seems to drop a few degrees in temperature.

Jayden finally speaks. "Guardians, here? Why should we believe a stranger..." He points at Micah, who tenses the bow already knocked in his grasp. "A traitor, and two girls," He spits that word, then continues, "who disobey their leader's commands at every possible chance they get?" The room hums with agreement.

Leah takes this as her cue to back me up: "I never betrayed you, Jayden, so just calm the hell down." She rolls her eyes and lets out an audible breath as if she were talking to a two-year-old.

Skyler and I shoot each other looks of disbelief at her new-found confidence. I can't deny I'm kind of enjoying watching Jayden be out-sassed.

"I was captured by them: Guardian Hunters. The lowest rung of Guardians that are intent to prove themselves to the Chosen. Micah saved me from them and we returned the favour to Skyler and Ava. They have an informant, right here in the Resistance. They know our location and they know how many of us are here. Something called Red Game was mentioned. And it's going to happen at dawn," Leah says.

Ryder interjects, alarm escalating on his handsome features. "Red Game is a code word that we were taught as Guardians. It means 'explosion'."

"They mean to blow this place up, with everyone in it. And come in with ground support to finish the job. Today," I say.

The room descends into anarchy.

"Nice job," Skyler says sarcastically.

Yeah, ok. Maybe waltzing into a room and telling people they are going to be blown up probably wasn't the most strategic of plans.

"It needed to be done," Leah says as she places a hand on my shoulder. "It'll shock them into action rather than spending time deciding whether they can trust us or not."

As if on cue, Jayden resumes control of the room: "Quiet!" he shouts. "We are soldiers and we can handle this situation. They could be lying. How do we know they are telling the truth? All three of them can't be trusted. And the other ones, we don't even know."

Micah's back stiffens and the boys behind him shift uncomfortably but say nothing.

"You really wanna wait to find out right now? Play a little game of chicken?" Skyler says.

"And you're not soldiers, Jayden. If you think you are, you're deluded," Leah says, forcefully. "You've kept half of this room in the dark about how to protect themselves and the other half just go on small hunts and scout the area. You and Ryder say you're soldiers, but you haven't trained them the way they need to be trained. If you had any idea how strong Haven has become you would not be running a rebellion like this."

She says exactly what I have been thinking all this time but have been too scared to admit, to anyone else. These people are not ready to fight; it would be a blood bath that would not fall in their favour.

Jayden jumps forward a few steps. Ryder and Kai both try to hold him back, but they are struggling. "I am trying to protect them!" he yells at Leah.

"And so am I," she retorts.

I take control of the situation, addressing the group: "Alright, every soldier in here! Check every place you can in this building! Now, we've got a heads-up on the bomb. We can find it and disable it or we can move out of the building and find another safe place to hide. But trust me, for a group this size, half of you would die out there before the winter is out and we find a place as as fortified and protected as this. It's your choice."

And just like that, I am in control. Every able-bodied man and woman disperses. They shout to each other, giving directions of possible locations as to where a bomb could be hidden. I glance to Leah on my left, and Skyler on my right, and nod grimly at each of them. The three of us have firmly removed Jayden from leadership for now. Leah grins at Jayden in victory, and he gives us one final sour look before storming off.

And that's when Ryder lunges for Kai.

"Hey!" Leah yells, running to his aid. Skyler, Micah and I follow the scuffle that has broken out. Kai is clearly losing, pinned under Ryder's weight, Ryder punching him again and again.

I reach for Ryder and try to yank him off. I don't make much progress, so Skyler comes to my aid. "Ryder, what are you doing?!" I scream.

"He's the one that started this mess in the first place! He put us in danger, he lied to us! What if he's the traitor? What if he planted the bomb? He could tell us where it is."

Kai splutters, spitting out blood, fear etched all over his face. "I swear, Ryder. I wouldn't..."

"Well funnily enough Kai, your word no longer means all that much to me mate," he spits.

"Stop, both of you. *Stop,*" I command. The room quietens. Ryder and Kai look at me. The former in rage, the latter with a little gleam of hope in his eyes. Leah, Micah and Skyler hold them in place, just in case another fight breaks out.

"Kai is a *good person.* I know he would never put innocent people's lives in danger. He is not helping them do this. I trust him still. It isn't him, Ryder. What he did, he did it to protect his friend from harm. He did it to protect Leah." Kai's eyes swim with tears. "I would do the same for Skyler and you know it. So, if he's a traitor, then I am too." I pointedly step between them, blocking Kai from his view.

His features contort into disbelief. I don't think he expected me to defend Kai, after all he'd done. Until, with a low sigh, he finally concedes: "We don't have time for this right now. Skyler, stay with Kai. Keep an eye on him. Leah and Micah, take a patrol, we need to be watching for an attack at any time. Ave, you're with me."

Kai attempts a grateful smile. My face gives nothing away as I turn on my heel and leave. I glance back, just once to see him kneeling on the ground, his head hanging low in defeat.

FORTY-TWO

After an hour of searching, hysteria sets in. Crying and shouting begins as the reality of not knowing when the bomb might go off increases. Most try to remain calm, searching through the halls and rooms, methodically and quickly.

"If they are sending ground troops to finish the job, the explosion must only be strong enough to destroy part of the building, not all of it. The bomb they've got in here must be relatively weak," Ryder says.

I nod silently as we continue our search through the halls. I hope he's right. I notice a few of the group – no one whose name I remember among them – quietly packing their belongings when they think no one is looking. I see three or four of them, bags in tow, disappearing into the tree line.

Jayden looks exasperated when I tell him but nods reluctantly. "The Resistance will not become Haven," he says, almost to himself. "People are free to leave the group when they want to."

For the third time, I inspect the women's dormitories. My muscles creak as I drop down to the floor, wriggling under the beds, checking for abnormal possessions in all of the women's things. My chest feels tight as I remember the voice I heard over the radio. The voice that must have come from someone in the Resistance.

Someone in here. Someone in this building wants to kill us.

As I check under the final bed I hear someone enter the room. The knot in my chest loosens a little as I see who it is. His face is expressionless as his eyes travel over my body slowly.

"Remember the last time in here?" Ryder says with a grin. "We should do that again sometime – minus the tying up, of course. Or with it. I mean, whatever you prefer." The smile he gives makes my knees shake a little, but he continues the search, lifting all of the beds up to check underneath.

We search everywhere, tearing clothes from the one wardrobe we shared, tearing up mattresses, everywhere we could think of. I attempt to rip up the pillow I'd just picked up, failing miserably. He takes it off me and finishes the job like it was a piece of paper. "What's wrong? You're weaker again."

I snort at his comment but stick to the task at hand. "Got drugged by the Hunters with the same injections they use in Haven. I think it was a stronger strain, though," I say, wiping the sweat collecting on my brow. My legs feel shaky, despite having travelled here on Leah's back.

And then Ryder is directly in front of me, blocking my path. I am unable to move anyway. He is scorching with me with his gaze. "You're not safe here," he says softly.

"Neither are you," I counter.

"You should go; take Skyler. Get away from here. You need to stay alive for your family."

"I'm not leaving. Not while all these people's lives are at stake."

His eyes abandon my face all too quickly. I am disarmed at his sudden anger. But I see it for what it is: a tactic to get me to cut and run.

I grab onto his shudders and hold him at arm's length. "Look, I'm not going anywhere no matter what you do, ok? There's nowhere else I've got to go." I gasp and squeeze my eyes shut as inspiration hits me.

The bomb. It had to be somewhere no one would go.

"Ava, what is it?"

"I—I think I know where the bomb is. It's got to be where it can ruin the building easily, trapping people inside. And it's got to be where no one would go. Where no one would find it easily. Everyone goes everywhere in the building. Except from one spot."

Ryder's eyes light up with the answer, pulling me towards the door. "It's on the roof."

FORTY-THREE

Time is a strange thing. You always feel like you've got too much of it until you don't have enough. Ryder and I sprint through the halls together, my hand in his. He drags me along, as fast as my legs can carry and we burst through the entrance and outside into the courtyard. There isn't enough time in the world to prepare me for what I see next.

The Hunter Guardians who captured us are here, attacking the Resistance with every piece of artillery possible. Everywhere I look I see fighting. Gunshots echo for miles around. I hear shrill screams and cries of fear. The grass is wet with blood. The Resistance are fighting fiercely. But they can only get a clear shot at taking one of them down when they are close enough to disarm the Hunter Guardians. They sprint, jump and kick in the air, wielding their own weapons. Thankfully, their reactions are so fast they are often able to dodge and move from the bullets. But often just isn't enough. Machine guns mow them down, the sheer amount of bullets impossible for anyone to avoid.

I see Leah and Skyler and Jayden and Kai out there in the flurry of bodies fighting the Guardians.

I see Micah shooting his bow from a nearby tree.

I see an older man, just not quick enough, hit square in the chest.

It is utter turmoil. Bloody chaos. Horrific doesn't begin to describe the scene before me. I look up through my shock to find Ash standing on a truck, mowing down a woman with a machine gun. I am pulled back roughly, my arm socket screaming in protest.

"You can't help them: you're too weak."

"But—"

"Focus, Ava. What is going to help them more? If that thing goes it'll collapse and everyone still inside will die. All the children are still in there, Ava. We need to get onto the roof."

I nod numbly, too petrified to speak. Ryder lifts me up to the first rung of the ladder. We climb. As the roof comes into sight, I see something small and black and out of place attached to the other side of the wall. I turn to offer my hand to him and he grunts gratefully, lifting his hand up to mine. I feel a whoosh of air as a bullet sails past my face. Ryder leaps on me, knocking me onto the concrete, blocking my body from the shots. "Thanks," I say.

We wriggle along the rooftop toward the black box, bullets flying all around us. When we get to the bomb, Ryder tries to lift it, to no avail. It's been stuck onto the roof. The numbers are red and they read: 1:59.

"Ryder—"

"I know," he grunts.

"Get off the roof," he says. "I've got it. You need to go." He doesn't look up as he examines the coloured wires, trying to trace them to the source.

"No," I say. "I'm not leaving you here, so shut up. Let me help." There are three wires running along and around the black box: yellow, black, and red. "Why don't you cut all three?" I ask.

"That will set it off. We learnt about these as Guardians, I just can't remember..."

"Are you serious?!" I almost yell. "You've been taught how to disarm one, but you don't *remember*?"

He grabs the knife from his shoe. "I'm pretty sure it's the red one."

He's *pretty* sure?

"I trust you," I say, praying to anyone that's listening that my faith is in the right person.

Ryder looks at me once more before turning his attention to the wire. He cuts it as fast as he can. The numbers stop. Nothing happens.

He was right.

We turn and lie on our backs, our lungs heaving.

"Ryder," I smile. "You did it. We're safe."

"Not yet."

I look down and still see Hunter Guardians still attacking. Despite their obviously superior strength and speed, the Resistance are getting tired. "Have you got a gun?" I say to Ryder. He pulls one from his pocket. We look at each other with dread. We both know what must be done. I'd rather this on my conscience than his. I see Tex take one down, and Kai take another. I try to take the gun from his grasp.

"No." He pulls it back. "I can do it."

He takes a deep breath. He locates the first Guardian from his vantage point. This one is fighting Tex. He shoots and the man falls to the floor.

The next man is fighting Kai. As the man falls I see Kai look up in confusion, searching for his saviour. But we are so hidden from view up here that he can't see us. He runs to help Skyler who is fighting another dark-haired female Guardian. But he is too late as the next Guardian falls to the floor, unmoving. One by one, Ryder takes them down. None of them can detect where the bullets are coming from; we are too well hidden.

Each bullet makes my ears ring. I count all six in my mind. We hear silence from below as the fighting ceases. They have no one left to fight.

When he is done, Ryder turns from his vantage point and slides down to sit beside me. He looks at me. His face is stone cold, daring me to judge him.

"We do what we have to, to survive – right?" I say. "You protected your people. There's no shame in that."

His face crumples in relief at my understanding of what he has just done. I hold him as his body convulses with sobs. I kiss a tear from his cheek. "It's ok," I say, the mantra I've told myself a thousand times. But now it is for the comfort of another. "You're ok."

FORTY-FOUR

Leah throws Ash onto the ground. Ash tries not to wince as she kneels, her hands bound tightly together. Leah had caught her in the woods, running away from the fight, just before Ryder had started shooting at them from the rooftop. Luckily for her. Or unluckily. I'm yet to decide.

"Look who's the prisoner now," Leah says, seeming to take a little too much pleasure in Ash's attempts to get up from the ground, knocking her down every time. The remainder of the Resistance gathers around us and I do a quick headcount. About fifty are left. Fewer than twenty Guardians had taken down almost half of us. We'd lost fifty soldiers in the space of less than ten minutes. I shudder to think what the hundreds of Guardians back at Haven would have done to us.

Skyler runs towards me. "Are you hurt?" I ask. She shakes her head. Lucy, the girl she had been spending so much time with lately, is looking toward Skyler anxiously. "Go." I smile. Skyler nods and runs to Lucy, embracing her fiercely. I always knew Skyler was a strong fighter and that Kai or Leah wouldn't let anything happen to her, but through the fighting I hadn't been able to stop the worry gnawing at my insides.

"Ash is the only one left. Micah picked off any of the ones fleeing. We owe that win to him. And Ryder. Wasn't he great? Because of them, the Doctor doesn't know our location. From what you said Ava, they were only going to let him in on the plan when it was finished, so they'd get all the credit for taking down the Resistance." Leah rattles off the information without looking away from Ash.

I glance behind me briefly to Ryder. His eyes are glued to me, his expression triumphant over what we have just achieved. But there's something else there, something that looks a lot like grief. And under the triumphant facade, I know that he is seeing the faces of those Guardians. I know that it will haunt him for the rest of his life. People are coming over to him, smiling, hugging, patting him on the back in gratitude. One "thank you" after another for saving their home and their lives.

A cackle from Ash shakes us all from the moment. Micah draws his bowstring taut, aiming it directly for her face. Jayden waves him away. "You have no idea what's coming, do you?" she spits at us. "You're idiots for thinking you could ever destroy Haven. And you –" She turns to me. "You could have had everything you ever wanted. The Doctor was prepared to give it to you, but now you've joined them?" She gestures to the ragged group around us, "He's coming for you, Ava."

I grip my knife tighter in my hand at the threat and make my way over to her. "If he doesn't know where I am, he can't come for me. And you're the last person who knows." I clutch her hair, revealing her neck and pulling the blade to it. "So I guess you're shit out of luck."

She snarls at me. "You won't kill me. You need to know what he wants from you. And I'm the only one here who knows. And I've decided that I don't want to tell you just yet. I want a bargain."

"I'll beat it out of you then," I snarl back. I pull back for the first blow.

"Ava!" Skyler reprimands.

I pause mid-air. Sense pours into me. I look around at the faces in front of me. Kai looks slightly nauseous at what I am about to do, his heart so big, so pure. The others look uneasy at my sudden aggression. Ryder is the only one who stares back coolly. He's letting me do what needs to be done.

"Wait," Jayden commands. "She's valuable. We need her safe for now. Ryder, take Ash away. Find a cell for her. Ava, we need to talk. Come with me."

I drop Ash's head and stalk off after him.

"Ava?" I hear Kai's voice behind me.

"We'll talk later, Kai," I mutter, not even turning around.

FORTY-FIVE

"This place is beautiful," I say as we continue to walk along the cliff line. It was only a five-minute walk from the observatory to here. The cliff is vast and majestic, the rocks spilling out from the sheer drop onto the crashing waves hundreds of feet below. I can't believe I haven't found this place before; the view from the cliff makes me feel like I'm back at home.

"Isn't it?" Jayden says. "I come out here to think, to cool down. I figured you could use that." Jayden eyes me with a look that I can't quite interpret. I blush a little.

"Yes, I guess I could, couldn't I? I'm sorry for losing my temper. But that girl, she just ... She's everything I hate about Haven." In the silence that follows, my mind wanders to Xander and Dad. I wonder how they are, if they'd found a safe place yet; or if Xander's hunting skills have improved. "But yeah," I continue. "You were right to pull me out of that situation. I'm sorry. I think I scared a few of the soldiers." We chuckle as we begin to move closer to the cliff's edge.

"Yeah, just a bit."

We are quiet for a moment.

"We need to talk about the mole in the Resistance," I say finally, glad to have something to discuss that feels like we're making progress, past the anger I feel towards Ash and the other attackers. "Who could have been leaking information to the other Hunter Guardians to orchestrate the attack?"

I stand next to Jayden, staring out towards the grey sea. I fidget slightly, exhaustion overcoming my body. I sit down on the soft grass, and Jayden joins me. I am suddenly cold, the wind seeping through my clothes into my bones. I shiver unexpectedly. The rush of adrenaline has left my body. I feel like I'm settling into whatever comes next – after the battle.

"Yeah. We should talk about that sometime soon." Something in his voice seems distant. We've both had a pretty rough day.

"I can't believe it's all come to this. After the Cull, all the Mutes destroying whatever we have left. You'd think we'd band together, you know? Not still be fighting each other," I say.

"Well, that's the human race for you. Destructive till the end. I can see where they're coming from," he continues. "In a way."

"How do you mean?" I ask.

"Imagine you knew your fate: you were to die like the majority of the population already have, but you have the power to stop that from happening. I've gotta hand it to the Chosen and the Doctor – they're self-made men."

I give him an incredulous glance. "He's a monster."

A pause.

"Perhaps. But we have to be monsters to survive, now."

"Perhaps," I agree. He looks at me.

I feel uncomfortable. I can't pinpoint why; something feels strange. I shift a little and stand up. I move to walk back towards the forest. "We should probably head back now. Thanks for helping me cool down out here. It's a nice spot." I say.

Instantly Jayden is in front of me, blocking my path back to the forest. He steps forward, tilting his head, just an inch. "I don't think that's necessary," he says.

I try to sidestep him again, but he is too fast for me. I feel the power and tension in his muscles from my position a few paces away, and I realize I am bare, without weapon or recourse against him. The dart has still taken all of my strength from me. Physically, I am no match for him. He smirks again as if he knows my very thoughts as they click into place.

Oh my God.

"You're the asshole that betrayed everyone, aren't you?"

"First prize to you," he says darkly.

He is advancing towards me, one step at a time. I am forced to retreat back in order to counter him. I glance behind me and sense his intention: we are slowly heading towards the precipice of the cliff. He's blocking me off from being able to run anywhere. He wants me with no options.

I need to try and stall him, to keep him talking until I can figure a way out of this mess. I'd *let* him take me here. Shit, I had been *so* stupid. "B—but why? You're the leader of the Resistance. You're Ryder's brother!"

Suddenly, so much becomes clear to me. The radio conversation with Ash when we were captured by the Hunters. Why Jayden has been so against teaching the Resistance how to fight – as long as they were weak, they would rely on him and his judgement. Even though he'd been planning their deaths with the Hunter Guardians all this time.

He'd fooled us all.

"Thomas was an idealist. Ryder is too – has been all his life. I'm the realist. There is no surviving out here in the wild. It's impossible.

It's either death-by-Mute, or a life of slavery with the Chosen. I am *not* going to be Marked again." He spits. "I had to adapt. I had to make myself valuable to the Chosen and the Doctor, to do him a favour. To save him from what he's terrified of: the Resistance to his cause."

"You wanted to hand the Resistance over to him, so he could enslave or kill them. So he would be indebted to you. So, he'd make you a Chosen too."

"Smart girl."

"You're a coward. People like you are what is keeping people like White Suit in power. If you led the Resistance properly, you could've beat them. We could have all been safe."

"Nowhere is safe anymore, Ava. I'm doing what I have to do to survive. My plans shifted when the Hunter Guardians found us, so I had to make a deal with them."

I can't hear any more of his madness. I attempt a punch. He catches it mid-air with the palm of his hand, slowly squeezing down on my knuckles. Pain shoots through me and I scream in agony. I kick him as hard as I can. He doesn't even blink.

"But you, Ava. He wants you alive. Think of how he would reward me if I gave him the ultimate prize, *and* if I wiped out the entire Resistance for him. I'd be more than a Chosen, I'd be *the* Chosen. He would give me anything I wanted." He smiles at the thought.

He drags me further towards the forest, back where we've come from, and I kick and scream more, desperate for anything to slow him down. He clamps a hand on my mouth. His strength is making me feel dizzy and weak. I feel myself beginning to pass out.

Then, there's sudden movement on my left. It all happens so fast I can't even begin to imagine how it is possible. Someone tackles him to the ground and Jayden lets go of my hand. Another hand replaces his, grabbing my wrist and stopping my scream outright.

Kai pulls me up to my feet as fast as possible. With lightning speed he is up again, rounding on Jayden. But there is another figure there, too – tussling with Jayden next to the cliff. I make out Skyler's blonde hair and my lungs forget how to work.

Kai launches himself forward when he sees I am unharmed. "Kai, NO!" He can't even fight – he's going to get himself killed. He lunges at Jayden but is quickly knocked down.

"KAI!" I scream. He is not moving. The force of the hit has knocked him unconscious.

Skyler and Jayden are circling one another, each attempting to land a deadly blow. Knives have been drawn; they slash at each other. Jayden's cut hits home on Skyler's leg, splitting her trousers and skin open in a flash of red. She yells in pain.

I grab the largest tree branch I can lift and run toward Jayden, ready to hit him, poke his eye out, anything that can give Skyler the upper hand. The branch breaks on him as if it were a twig. I swing my leg out to unbalance him. Even without my power, I've still got technique. But it's as if I'm merely a fly. He swots me away, sending me flying.

Skyler is fast and has the technique, but Jayden is too strong. She's already tiring and beginning to make mistakes. One costs her a series of punches in the gut, which forces her back closer towards the cliff, reeling from the pain.

"Hold it." A voice I could never mistake.

Ryder emerges from the tree line, a gun pointing directly at Jayden's head. "It's done, Jayden."

"Ryder, listen to me. Come with me. We can have all we ever wanted. We just need to give them her. *Ryder.*" He is begging Ryder to see sense.

"No." Ryder's jaw tenses, his finger twitching.

"Ryder," he continues. "Thomas was crazy to think he could ever beat them or be free of them. No one can destroy Haven. We can't beat the Chosen. We have to join them. And she's our ticket." He nods to-wards where I'm standing. "Come on. You think Mum gave her life for us to sit around and do nothing? For us to just become slaves again like she was? Because that's where we're headed if we don't hand her back to the Doctor. She sacrificed herself, so we can have a better life. And I'm making one for us right now."

Ryder's hands are shaking with the gun in them. He grimaces in pain at the mention of his mother. I hear Kai groan as he gains con-ciousness, and slowly move toward him. If Jayden goes for him, he has nothing to protect himself with.

Jayden's voice is as sweet as honey: "Anything we want, we could have. No more running, no more hiding. We would have safety, a roof over our heads, anything we want. Come on, brother."

He's stepping closer to Kai who is near the cliff: his only way out now. I, too, have moved to Kai, trying to force him behind me. I gesture for Kai to step away, but his eyes are locked elsewhere, away from me. I anticipate the move as quickly as it comes, and I fling myself in front of Kai just in time. The knife headed for his heart is thrust upwards by my kick.

I duck the punches Jayden throws my way. Kai springs to my aid. And we are trapped in a deadly dance, one that moves too quickly for Ryder to pinpoint with his aim. And then Kai is down on the ground; blood is everywhere. I scream for him, distracted for a moment.

Jayden has me by the neck. My throat is crushed under his fingers; I am drowning all over again. He lifts me in the air and my body shud-ders in pain. It is unbearable. My consciousness begins to fade in and out, numbing me, if only for a moment.

"You can't kill your own brother, Ryder! It's not in you," Jayden yells towards Ryder.

"Let me leave or I'll kill her right now. Don't think I won't. Me. Or. Her."

I can make out Ryder's eyes. They look certain as he aims for Jayden's shoulder. "It's always her," Ryder says, and then he shoots.

The shot rings out loud and clear as does Jayden's yell of pain. I am released instantly, and I gasp in a few breaths of air, placing a hand on my bruised throat. Jayden stumbles back in shock a few steps, then he freezes, clutching his wound on his shoulder blade.

I see it before it happens: a small rock that is the difference between safety and danger for him.

"No!" I cry out, my throat scratchy and hoarse. I try to leap forward, to alert Kai, to make him help me. I hear Ryder cry out too. But he's too far away to save Jayden from the fall. He's yelling to Kai, the closest of all of us to Jayden, imploring him to help his brother.

Kai doesn't move.

He just watches impassively as Jayden disappears over the cliff.

FORTY-SIX

I stand amongst the graves of Guardians and Resistance alike as dawn breaks. The day after the attack has been a complete blur, a hazy memory that I'm merely watching, not living in. Faces of people now gone from this world fade in and out of focus. I sit down on the grass and begin to rip it from the ground absentmindedly, letting the individual blades fall from my fingers. I lie down with all my brothers and sisters below.

"Human nature, isn't it? The need to destroy," Ryder says, appearing behind me, gesturing to the ruined grass around me. He sounds eerily like his brother. I try to ignore the thought, but it seeps away into my bones.

I drop the grass from my palm, still looking upwards towards the sky. I make no effort to stand up. "What do you want, Ryder?" I sigh. "You haven't even looked at me since " I trail off as I see the mere thought of his brother's loss makes his face crumple in despair. I can't bring myself to say Jayden's name. Not yet.

Ryder frowns and shakes his head, lowering himself to sit by me.

"I know, I'm sorry. I've been trying to get the courage to do this."

"To do what?" I ask.

"To finish this. To let you go."

And just like that, my palms become sticky and my heart sinks into the grass below me.

He continues: "Since the fight I just haven't been able to ... talk to you. The truth is when we were up on that roof when we were disarming the bomb I wasn't scared for myself, or for the people fighting for their lives below," He swallows. "I was only scared about you. About losing you."

"And that's my problem. Beating the Chosen. *Punishing* them for what they have done. It's everything to me. My mother, Thomas, and now Jayden. That ... Doctor has taken everything from me and I need to repay the debt, or I can't move on from it, from what he's done. Or their sacrifice was for nothing." He is placing tiny daggers in me, twisting them a little more with every word.

"I need to end this, and if I let myself be with you ... it splits my focus. That needs to be the most important thing: the fight. You can't be." He pauses before he plants the final dagger dead centre. "You no longer are."

I am desperate to get away and to slap him and to bury my face in his chest all at the same time. But I just ... sit there. I want to tell him I still care, that we can fight them together, but I just ... sit there, not even looking at him.

I hear myself say, "I agree."

"What?" His voice rises, as if he was expecting my temper would kick in, as if he was expecting me to fight for him, to beg him not to leave, to tell him he's wrong.

"You're completely right. There's no space in this war for love. Only survival."

And I hate that these words are coming out of my mouth.

And I hate that he had to tell me he no longer wanted me to see sense.

"I've played along with your *Resistance*. I get that Haven has taken everything from you. But not from me. My family are still out there. And I've let you distract me from them, all this time."

His mouth opens and closes, as if this wasn't the reaction he expected. But it doesn't stop me wanting him. I've always wanted him. I think I've just been too stubborn to admit it. The warmth of his smile, the teasing looks when our eyes met after our kiss, our conversations in Haven that made me want to fight to stay alive.

He looks at me and I see that the connection has been severed. There's something pressing hard on my chest. "So, I guess this is good-bye then." he says.

"It is. Skyler and I will be out of your way by dawn." I turn to leave.

"Ave – I... I still love you. I just can't love you right *now*." His voice is panicked, he's begging me to see his point of view.

"That's the thing Ryder," I whirl around, "I don't know much about love – but when you truly love someone, it's not a *choice*."

I don't let him reply. I turn, and I run. I run and I don't look back at the man I've just left in the graveyard. I run until I can't breathe anymore. But the pain of what Ryder has just said won't go away. I've put my family second to the Resistance for too long. I've ignored what my mother told me to do: to protect them at all costs. And I've failed. And now, they are gone from our home and I have no idea where to even begin. This land is *massive*. They could be anywhere on it right now, and I have no way to track them.

I look out to the city of Wellington below, now ravaged beyond repair. It's probably the most dangerous place you could ever go. Mutes always hang around there, waiting for humans to come back into the city to find much needed supplies. But if you were smart enough, if you had the right hiding place, the right supplies... It's somewhere no one would ever follow you.

It's probably the most dangerous place they could've chosen.

So I guess I'll start there.

ACKNOWLEDGEMENTS

The cliché: I don't know where to begin, is in fact, so true at this point in time. So let's start at the very beginning (a very good place to start, says Julie Andrews).

To my parents, your constant flow of support and love means the world to me. Your utter belief and pride in me is astounding. Thank you for being you.

To my big brother, to whom I have always admired and attempted to imitate throughout my entire life, thank you for being worthy of looking up to.

I began writing this book at nineteen years old, when I was studying at university. Thank you to everyone there for inspiring my creativity: staff and students alike. Some of whose names I have commandeered for the purpose of this book, and whom many of the characters are influenced by. That point in my life was a source of both great pain, and joy. But without experiencing that dichotomy at such a young age, this book would not be what it is today.

Thank you so much to my amazing friends, for always supporting and loving me. (You know who you are).

Pete, I love you. You are my best friend. Thank you for teaching me that love isn't fragile. It should be constant and without conditions. And with you, it is.

Thank you to Ashley Wyrick and Lisa Edwards. I enjoyed working with both of you so much and cannot wait to work with you again. Thank you for helping me translate what was in my head to the page with your incredible skills.

Thank you to Danna Mathias, who created this *amazing* cover and formatted the book for me. You were so great to work with.

And finally, thank you, dear reader, for picking up this book and choosing this story. It means more to me than you could ever know.

Love and light to you, dear friends.
E.J

Printed in Great Britain
by Amazon